MAKRA CHORIA

Borgo Press Books by Ardath Mayhar

The Absolutely Perfect Horse: A Young Adult Novel (with Marylois Dunn)
The Body in the Swamp: An Occult Mystery
Carrots and Miggle: A Novel of East Texas
The Clarrington Heritage
Closely Knit in Scarlatt
Crazy Quilt: The Best Short Stories of Ardath Mayhar
Deadly Memoir
Death in the Square
The Door in the Hill: A Tale of the Turnipins
The Dropouts: A Tale of Growing Up in East Texas
Feud at Sweetwater Creek: A Novel of the Old West
The Fugitives: A Tale of Prehistoric Times
The Heirs of Three Oaks: A Novel of the Old West
High Mountain Winter: A Novel of the Old West
How the Gods Wove in Kyrannon: Tales of the Triple Moons
Hunters of the Plains: A Novel of Prehistoric America
Island in the Lake: A Novel of Native America
Khi to Freedom: A Science Fiction Novel
The Lintons of Skillet Bend: A Novel of East Texas
Lone Runner: A Novel of the Old West
Lords of the Triple Moons: A Science Fantasy Novel: Tales of the Triple Moons
Makra Choria: A Novel of High Fantasy
Medicine Dream: Being the Further Adventures of Burr Henderson
Messengers in White: A Science Fantasy Novel
Monkey Station: A Novel of the Future (Macaque Cycle #1; with Ron Fortier)
People of the Mesa: A Novel of Native America
A Planet Called Heaven: A Science Fiction Novel
Prescription for Danger: A Novel of the Old West
Reflections; & Journey to an Ending: Collected Poems
A Road of Stars: A Fantasy of Life, Death, Love, and Art
Runes of the Lyre: A Science Fantasy Novel
The Saga of Grittel Sundotha: A Science Fantasy Novel
The Seekers of Shar-Nuhn: Tales of the Triple Moons
Shock Treatment: An Account of Granary's War
Slewfoot Sally and the Flying Mule: Tall Tales from Cotton County, Texas
Soul-Singer of Tyrnos: A Fantasy Novel
Strange Doings in the Pine Hills: Stories
Through a Stone Wall: Lessons from Thirty Years of Writing
Timber Pirates: A Novel of East Texas (with Marylois Dunn)
Towers of the Earth: A Novel of Native America
Trail of the Seahawks: A Novel of the Future (Macaque Cycle #2; with R. Fortier)
The Tulpa: A Novel of Fantasy
Two-Moons and the Black Tower: A Novel of Fantasy
Vendetta
Warlock's Gift: Tales of the Triple Moons
The World Ends in Hickory Hollow: A Novel of the Future
A World of Weirdities: Tales to Shiver By

MAKRA CHORIA

A Novel of High Fantasy

by

Ardath Mayhar

THE BORGO PRESS

An Imprint of Wildside Press LLC

MMIX

CONTENTS

FOREWORD

Perhaps the most destructive—of self as well as of other matters—desire of humankind is the need for power. It reveals, as Ayn Rand said in *The Fountainhead*, a second-hander, one who lives only by seeing his reflection in the eyes and behavior of others. This is a story about power and one who was wise enough to relinquish it.

—Ardath Mayhar
Chireno, Texas
October 2007

ABOUT THE AUTHOR

The author of sixty-two books, more than forty of them published commercially, **ARDATH MAYHAR** began her career in the early eighties with science fiction novels from Doubleday and TSR. Atheneum published several of her young adult and children's novels. Changing focus, she wrote westerns (as **Frank Cannon**) and mountain man novels (as **John Killdeer**), four prehistoric Indian books under her own name, and historical western *High Mountain Winter* under the byline **Frances Hurst**.

Recently she has been working with on-line publishers. *A Road of Stars* was her first original novel to appear in print-on-demand format. Many of her out-of-print titles are now available from e-publishers fictionwise.com and renebooks.com; many other novels are being published by the Borgo Press Imprint of Wildside Press and Amazon.com.

Now in her seventies, Mayhar was widowed in 1999, after forty-one years of marriage, and has four grown sons. She now works at home, writing short fiction and nonfiction, and doing book doctoring professionally. Her web pages can be found at:

w2.netdot.com/ardathm/ and
http://ofearna.us/ books/mayhar.html

CHAPTER ONE

The Makralo of Sherath stood upon the ancient platform, a half step above the level of the cobbled street. His people were crowded about him, and there was no armed guard nearer than the gateway to his house, some yards along the way. It was the yearly judging, a tradition that his most distant forefathers had instituted when Sherath was only a collection of mud huts in the middle of a vast forest.

Now the city stood, proud and elaborate, about its ruler. Stone houses with porches and balconies, shops with fine goods from Algonath and Sparrv and Elidion, and trade stalls with fresh produce from the farmers in the lush valleys that his sires had cleared and planted spoke of the city's wealth.

Choria, his younger daughter, watched from the window of her room. She was filled with pride in her father. He was so tall, so assured, even as those in the street approached, one by one, and lifted the spear from its slot in the stone. Each citizen took spear in hand and touched it to his ruler's throat. Had he ruled ill, troubled his people and their affairs unjustly, one or another would have thrust the glittering spear-point home. There would have been no punishment. That was the reason for the judging. It kept the rulers of Sherath reasonable and moderate in their use of the great power entrusted to them.

How great that power was few in the throng guessed,

Choria thought. Even she, just now learning the uses and controls of her own heritage, was amazed and sometimes appalled at the Gift that ran through her blood. She was learning to recognize in herself those impulses that she had been warned about. And to quell them.

"The Gift of the Makraitis is a burden as well as a blessing," her father had told her many times as they rode in the forest or inspected fields and herds. "There have been those of our kind who fell to temptation and misused it, injuring their folk and causing their own kindred to slay them. A taint runs at the root of our tree. In some generations, it crops out. My own brother was one—but he had the strength and the self-discipline to control it—until it became too great a burden. Then he cut his own throat with the spear as he stood on the Judgment Block. So well had he concealed his dark bent that his people wept and tore their garments when they saw what he had done."

There was something in that tale that made Choria shudder. Not only in the past did such things happen. Theora, her sister, the Heir of the Makralo, had her own dark traits.

Then, as Choria thought it, there came a step at the window of the room adjoining hers. The shutter was pushed back. Choria breathed as softly as possible, stepping farther back into the draperies. She had not the slightest wish to gain her sister's attention.

There was a snort from the window alongside. Then a whisper, sharp and decisive. "Thrust, you fool!"

Below, the woman so addressed merely caressed her ruler's throat with the spear-tip and dipped her curtsy before moving aside for the next comer.

Choria felt cold. Theora, even so young, already coveted their father's position. She would have him die unjustly, so that she might rule in his place. It was insane. Did she think a child of eleven would be allowed to rule? Another sound gave Choria the clue she needed to follow her sister's thought.

That was a rumbling clearing of the throat. *"Arr-hum!"* Their tutor, Glagio. If Theora had said what she did in his presence, it hinted at conspiracy, if not worse.

"When I am Makrala, I shall abolish the judgment. For myself, I will bring to the Block those who offend me during the year. That makes much more sense." Her childish voice didn't match the intensity of her words.

"A sensible intention," said Glagio. "But do not, I pray, utter it aloud to any but myself. Your father cannot disinherit you, but he might well have you killed, if he suspected your true intentions for Sherath."

"It will be my city, my country, when he is gone. I shall rule it as I will, and the Ring of the Makraitis will empower me. Who can stand against me, when I wear it upon my hand?"

"The Ring? It heals, I know. I have seen your father use it for that. I did not know that it held other powers," the tutor murmured. "Tell me more."

The child laughed. "You are not a Makraitis. You are not being trained in the uses of the family Gift. The Ring amplifies the intent of its wearer. If healing is that intent, if heals. If slaying is, then it slays instantly—except if its intended object is a member of the Family. I could bring down mountains upon Algonath, if I were properly placed and wished it with enough intensity."

Choria had wrapped herself totally in the velvet draperies of her window. Even though the solid wall stood between, she felt that her sister might sense her presence and know that she was listening. Though her father would not kill Theora, despite what Glagio had said, she had no doubt that her sister would arrange Choria's own death with less thought than she expended in choosing her own breakfast.

There came loud cheering from the street. Choria chose that time eagerly and fled her chamber, slipped

11

down the hallway, and stationed herself in her father's study. He would come soon.

She found herself shaking. Her teeth chattered. She hugged the cushion from Orinath's chair and huddled onto the stool beside it. Her world, dangerous always, had now turned dreadful. She knew that she must warn her father as soon as possible. She didn't really wish for Theora's death, but something must be done. At least, Glagio must go. He was encouraging her in the indulgence of her darker nature.

The cheering rose to hysterical intensity. It died away.

There was the clumping of metal-studded boots on the stone of the street, the pave of the courtyard. She rose, replacing the cushion and turning it so that that the tear spots didn't show. She stood waiting for her father, pale and red-eyed. She hoped that Theora, when she came, would attribute those signs to worry that some ill-balanced citizen might skewer their father in a fit of madness.

When Theora appeared in the doorway, Choria had regained control and was able to smile and nod. Her sister paid no attention. Choria had never been of interest to her, being unable to threaten her station as Heir.

Her disinterest was a very good thing, Choria had long ago decided.

CHAPTER TWO

Although Choria had access to her father at any time, except when he was closeted with important messengers or officials, it was not easy to find a time and place to speak with him privately. She knew as only a child can that the old house held many crannies useful to those who wanted to eavesdrop. She even knew the underground runs by which she could go out into the city secretly, though she never used them after finding where they led. No, she would not risk speaking out inside the House. She must wait until they were abroad in the forest or the fields.

Orinath knew his younger daughter extremely well. Her mother's death at her birth had left him with the burden of a double guilt. He had thought his wife mad, at one time. And he had begotten the child that killed her. He had taken Choria's rearing to heart, keeping her near him, teaching her himself, when time allowed. So it was not difficult to wheedle a ride with him when he went out to inspect the new western wall of the city. It was even less of a problem to persuade him to ride on into the forest, when that was done.

Only Garrier accompanied them. He was as near to a mother as Choria had ever known. She knew she could rest her life in his callused palms with all confidence. Once they had reached a quiet path amid the towering trees, she kneed her pony close to her father's big mount and looked up into his black eyes.

"I heard something, Father. Something I feel strange about telling you, but I think that you must know of it." She paused as he looked down quizzically, one gray-touched eyebrow quirked.

"Be certain it is nothing base, child," he said. "Nothing of tale-bearing for mischief's sake. That is one of the many faults our kind must be wary of."

She shook her head, feeling her long braid move against her back. "This is not tale-bearing, Father. It is the result of eavesdropping, though even that was not intentional. For that fault I will punish myself according to the rules. But you must know what it is that I heard." She looked down. Now that the time had come, she found it more than difficult to tell of the thing her sister had said.

However, it must be done. "When you stood on the Block, Theora came to her window. She did not know that I also stood at mine. She urged one of the citizens to thrust home the spear as it touched your neck. Then Glagio spoke. She told him that when she is made Makrala she will abolish the judgment for herself, instead bringing to the Block any who offend her. She said the Ring will enable her to do anything she chooses with Sherath, once she is ruler here."

She glanced up to see Orinath's dark brows draw together above his eyes. Garrier, on his other side, grunted and spat. The Makralo drew rein and dismounted, turning to lift his daughter from her saddle.

"The old traits still appear!" he said. "We will walk among the trees and talk of this, Choria. It is a thing I have not told you. You are so young—and yet you must know. There is no guarantee of the life of any man, far less that of a Makraitis. So...." He sighed and absently pulled a leaf from a trailing branch.

Garrier grunted again, then spoke. "It is better that she know, Lord. Tell her."

The leaf crushed between his tanned fingers. Then he

spoke. "When Theora was born, your mother tried to strangle her in her crib. All in our House thought her mad with that strange madness that sometimes comes to women who have just given birth. We safeguarded the child. Your mother came again to what we thought were her senses. But she refused to touch or tend her infant. In all else she was normal." He sighed.

"There was no lack of nurses. Theora thrived from the first, eating greedily, shrieking with all her might when anything went amiss. A normal baby, I was told. When I tried to reconcile the child with my wife, she smiled strangely and shook her head. Only at the end of her life did she speak of her."

Choria could see the pain in Orinath's eyes, the lines of his face. Never had he spoken to her of her mother. Now she was glad of it, if that memory was so painful to him.

"She said this: 'I have given to you a child worthy of you, at last. The other is of the Dark, Orinath. In her, the power of our kind has turned rotten and dangerous. I felt it even before her birth. She must be watched closely, compelled to study the ways of virtue. She will not embrace them voluntarily. I knew when she came from my womb what was best to do, but I was too weak to manage to kill her, and there were too many attendants.

"'When I had a chance, at last, I was prevented. Defy the Law, Orinath. Teach your worthy child the secrets of the Makraitis. Give Theora as little as you legitimately may, or less. Much less. She is a danger to all about her— and the terrible thing is that this is no fault of her own. Without the power, she might well be a normal and loving child. But no, she is as she is. Believe me, Orinath!'"

He sighed. "She stared into my eyes so intently, with such fervor, that I could not help but believe her. So I have taught you far more than is usual for one who is not the Heir. I have taught her less, though she does not know

15

that. She is sharp and suspicious. It has taken all my wit to deceive her as to the quality of her instruction. That is why I chose Glagio as her tutor. He is full of self-importance, yet too dense to understand what is being taught to his student."

Garrier said, "One without the Gift cannot see the quality of instruction in it. One without that instruction, even having the Gift, cannot judge her own progress. Theora believes herself the equal of any of the blood. I pray she continues to."

Orinath nodded. "But if she has already envisioned herself as Makrala, begun planning fundamental changes in the ways of Sherath—it is well that I know of it. Your mother was correct. All the worst traits of our power have surfaced again in her. It is time she went to the care of my sister, Ellida. That will remove her from you, and I fear for you if she realizes that you are being better taught than she. It also will part her from any in our household who might look to her as a source of influence, or as a tool to use in empowering themselves. She shall go to Ellida, when the snows on the passes melt."

He looked down at his hands and sighed. "There is a way to heal her, to remove the Gift that poisons her. Yet I, who know it, cannot use it; the Gift, in a ruling member of our family, will not operate so."

Choria felt a chill, as Garrier led up her pony and helped her to mount. With the two men, she turned back toward the city. The forest was full of spring. Birds and small beasts were busy with nest making and housekeeping. It should have been a joyful time. She would no longer need to walk softly and live in fear of her sister. Yet Choria was troubled.

If that cruel taint was in the Gift of the Makraitis, how might she be certain that it would not crop out in herself? How did one recognize the onset of the Dark? How had her mother known, as soon as she had, that Theora was

16

what she was?

How had her mother been so certain that her second child was clean of the taint? Another thought came to the child. She pulled in close to her father's horse again.

"What of the Ring?" she asked. "I know it is the talisman of the Makraitis. I know it enhances our own Gift. But could it do the things she believes it can do?"

Orinath laughed. There was no humor in the sound. "The Ring! She believes it to be invincible. Total power resides in it, she insists, even when I try to show her what the Ring truly is. She will not believe me. She wants a guarantee of omnipotence, but it is not and cannot be that."

He bent in his saddle to take his daughter's hand. "The Ring is a focus. It directs the thought of its wearer, if that wearer be Makraitis, toward the object of his thought. It concentrates his will upon his purpose. But it is the Gift that does the work, not the Ring. She deceives herself in that—and perhaps it is just as well. When one depends upon magic, one does not hone one's powers to their keenest edge."

A bird flew up in a dizzy circle before the horses, the notes of his spring song purling through the air. His wings made deep blue swirls against the greenery. Choria, relieved, gave herself up to enjoyment. Perhaps things would be all right, after all.

CHAPTER THREE

Theora raged. She made the House shudder with the violence of her anger. But she went, at last, to her aunt El-lida. Even those who supported her cause were relieved to see the last of her. And Choria celebrated her tenth birthday quietly with her father, uninterrupted by Theora's sly remarks and apparent ill will.

After that, the days went along evenly, turning themselves into weeks, weeks becoming months. Choria grew rapidly and learned even more rapidly. Every year, when time for judgment came, she remembered her sister and wondered how she fared in her exile. That recollection kept her attention focused, also, upon her inner self. She had a terror of growing to be like Theora.

It made her into a grim little person. The servants and tutors found her solemn and painstaking, lacking in merriment. Since she was not the Heir, they did what was required and took no more interest in her, which was a great relief. No monk in a cell examined his conscience more stringently than did the second daughter of the Makralo.

Her father noticed this and at his lessons he began to show her the wonders that were possible with the Gift: the healing of the sick, the enrichment of fields and flocks, the untwisting of the problems that troubled the minds of high and lowborn alike. He let her wear the Ring, at times, though that was an unprecedented thing.

He cautioned her continually. "The Ring is only a tool.

Do not depend upon it for more than it can give. Exercise your unaided will to its fullest. That is where our Gift lies, not in this gem-studded bauble."

Though the Ring helped her to find and to direct her own powers, she kept his words at the forefront of her mind. Once she had attained some mastery of the Gift, she no longer asked to wear the Ring. Her father, she knew, noted and approved.

On her fourteenth birthday he had the cooks pack a picnic. He and his daughter and Garrier rode to the forest, deep into the western reaches along the path leading to the distant hunting lodge they often visited. But they didn't have time for that long a journey, so they turned aside into a smooth green glade beside a pebbled stream.

Garrier unpacked the food, and they sat about and ate, laughing at quips and chance comments until there came a pause. Into that came a long sigh from Orinath.

"I have a gift for you, Choria. One that may make your life safer and easier. But I also have ill news. Which would you have first?"

She tossed her dark braid over her shoulder, her brown eyes alight. "The gift, first, oh please!"

He laughed. "Fourteen you may be, but you are still a child, thanks to the gods. The gift it is, then. May it aid and comfort you." He handed her a small packet wrapped in a bit of cloth-of-silver, pinned with a rose formed of pink quartz.

She unpinned the rose and set it into the collar of her somewhat crumpled tunic. The cloth unfolded readily, revealing a bracelet of strange glowing metal, set about with blood-red stones. It had an unearthly beauty, but it also had a look of power, leashed but ever-present. She looked up at her father. "It is no simple bauble," she said.

"No. It contains one of the gems from the Ring. I replaced it with another, like but less potent. Theora will never know. The metal came from Algonath, from the mines in the mountains, where metals of strange properties and gems of weird power come to light from time to time. With this upon your person, you will be totally immune to any impulse your sister might send through the Ring. Place it on your arm, above the elbow. It opens— see? Your sleeve will conceal it."

The circle opened along a thin wire when a catch was pressed. She slid it above her elbow. When it snapped shut again, the metal cooled to a dull silver. The red stones might have been enamel. It had no look either of power or of great value. Yet Choria felt a shiver go through her. It had its source in the bracelet.

She knew, then, that the second thing her father had offered must be the thing she had dreaded for almost five years. She bent her head and said, "Theora will return soon."

"The passes are clear. Ellida sent a messenger bird three days ago. The girl is ready, trained in all that my sister can teach her. It is time she returned to her city and began learning to rule it well. I can only pray that Ellida's teaching has corrected some of the twists in her nature."

Garrier harrumphed dubiously from the other side of the cloth spread between them. "I've misgivings, Lord. In a dream I have seen grave changes, terrible heavings of the ground and bubblings of waters. I have looked for you and never found you. It was an ill day when you prevented her mother from strangling her."

Orinath stood and reached down to pull Choria to her feet. "It was," he said. "But done is done. Nothing can alter that. We must watch our backs and our fronts as well, once she returns. I, too, doubt that Ellida's best efforts have made much change in my older daughter."

The ride back was silent. Choria would have been chilled with dread, if the bracelet had not been on her arm. From that spot warmth seemed to radiate, moving through her body, making her feel stronger than ever before in her life. She kneed the horse toward her father's tall mount and reached up to take his hand. He squeezed her fingers. The pair rode on, hand in hand, through the spring-dappled wood.

Her confidence didn't last. On the third day after Choria's birthday, Theora came home again after her long absence. She was now fifteen and a half, but she looked entirely a grown woman. She wore a woman's looped overskirt above her riding pantaloons, but more than any garment that clothed her, she seemed wrapped in layers of arrogance.

As Theora came up the steps of the House of the Makraitis, the servants waiting to greet her turned pale. Choria, waiting at the top with Orinath, felt her father tense beside her. Foreboding filled her as she felt those black eyes sweep across her to settle on the Makralo.

"Greeting, Father. My aunt also sends greeting. And gratitude for entrusting my training to her. She also sends a message. She says that you cheated me in my training and in the control of the Gift, which is rightfully mine. She has rectified that error—and more. She reminds you that your brother and hers managed to conceal his— aberration—from all. She asks me to inform you that she was also successful. She also concealed it." The tinkling laugh hurt Choria's ears.

Orinath didn't flinch. "Then I have made a terrible error in sending you to her. Meaning only the best, I have done what is worst for myself and my people. Yet you are my Heir. The Law stays my hand with regard to you. Think long before you make any rash move, however. There are other ways...."

She moved past him, still laughing, and entered the House. Choria took her father's hand in both her own, but neither said a word until they reached his study. Then he sat, and she took the stool at his knee. Heads close together, they spoke in whispers.

"Guard yourself, Father," Choria breathed. "I fear for you, now that she is at home again."

"I will do that. And more. I cannot, now, teach you the forbidden matters that are outside the Law, but I will make provision for you to learn them, if there should be need. Go softly, Choria. I do not want Theora to suspect that you might threaten her in any way. Keep close to Garrier. Guard him, and he will guard you. I am afraid for us to seem too close, now."

He rose and moved toward the doorway. She went through and up the corridor, feeling upon her back unseen gazes. She knew that ears had strained to hear what had been spoken privately, but she hoped that no one had been able to detect their soft tones.

At the head of the stair, she turned toward her room. Theora's maid stood in her way. "This is now the Heir's chamber, fittingly. It was her mother's. Go to the other wing, where the waiting women have their quarters. You will find a place made ready for you."

The saucy wench was challenging her to protest, but she recalled her father's words and said nothing. With a mild nod, she turned away and went to begin her new life in the shadow of her sister.

CHAPTER FOUR

The House of the Makraitis became a place of tumult and nerves. Theora was everywhere, reordering her father's household, turning out chambers long unused, rummaging in the archives after secret papers, making herself a pain to all involved. At last her father could bear no more and called her into his study.

Though the consultation was to be private, Choria now made use of her knowledge of the secret ways in the House. Wriggling her way between walls, she came to a niche built into a space between the study and the library beyond. Cobwebs assured her that this was one spot undiscovered as yet by her sister's spies. She settled to listen. Eavesdropping might be a serious fault, but in this case she felt compelled, for her own safety, to listen.

There was a small hole bored into a chink in the marble lining the study's wall. She knew it to be invisible from the other side, for she had searched for it. Setting her ear to this, she listened to the murmur of voices.

For once, Theora was neither whining nor shouting. Her voice was taunting. "There is nothing that you can do. I am the Heir. I am learning all that can be learned about my own House, my own country. The Law supports me in this, as you know all too well. I understand your feelings in the matter, make no mistake."

Orinath's deep tones vibrated through the room. "I do not object to your learning what it is fit for you to know.

But there is no need for you to disrupt the household, to upset and distress the servants, and to be impolite and demanding past any reasonable necessity. The Law may prevent my restraining your researches, but I am still your father. You are less than seventeen. I can punish you physically, and I will, if this continues. Remember that, Theora. My sister, whatever her faults, did not foster such ill-bred traits in you. That I know. I feel that she quelled your baser nature while you were with her, insofar as your personal behavior went. Now you are reveling in your freedom from her discipline. Am I not correct?"

There was a sulky silence. Then Theora's voice, sharp and almost fearful. "You would not dare!"

"I would, and I will. Ellida did, too, or I am even more mistaken in her than I thought. She made you behave decently in her household, did she not?"

"Yes." The syllable was grudging.

"I will not do less. And do not think that you can indulge your tempers on my staff. I will not allow it. Though you may be the Heir, I am Makralo. Do not forget that. The folk do not know the dark secrets of our kind. The gods have seen to it that not one who ever carried the taint has remained long in power. Remember that, daughter. I do not wish you ill. I only wish that I could wish you well."

There was a shrill laugh. "Do you, indeed? Unfortunately, it is not possible, and it could never be. I am one of the true Makraitis. You are a weak fool."

"One quite able to stripe your skin. Remember that, and behave accordingly."

There was a swish as the girl rose from her chair. Steps clipped toward the door. As Choria withdrew from her cranny, she heard her father give a long, deep sigh.

The next days demonstrated the effectiveness of his words, however. Theora went about her researches more quietly, without insulting or degrading those involved in

helping her. Choria stayed far from the scenes of her dep-
redations, haunting the stables or doubling her training
time in the small area given over to the Guard for that purpose.

There was no lack of partners there, for the officers
and men alike were proud of her progress in arms. Theora
had always scorned physical battle, thinking that her Gift
was enough to safeguard her person and her plottings.
Choria followed in the tradition of the more practical
women of her line. A blade knew no sex, when wielded by
a knowing hand. A bow sent an arrow where it was aimed,
if the aimer knew her craft. She intended to be armed in all
possible ways, when the time came that she must defend
herself and her country.

She returned to her room one evening, sweating and
dusty from the training yard, to find Theora waiting for her
in her chamber. Though she was surprised, she did not
show any unease at finding her sister there.

"Theora! Can you spare the time to visit a room where
there is no hope of finding a secret hiding place or arcane
helpers?"

Theora ignored her remark. "I have come to see what
sort of person you have become. If you are a threat, I will
have you killed, once our father is out of my way. If not, I
may let you go your way—or I may use you as trading
goods. Algonath has a young prince approaching mar-
riageable age. It is a rich country. An alliance might be to
my advantage."

Choria could hardly believe that her sister would be so
open about her aims. She heard her out silently, however,
while putting her corselet and boots away and donning a
thin robe. When the diatribe was done, she turned and
looked into Theora's eyes.

"Father bade me not to come blade-to-blade with you,
sister, but to go my own way quietly and without offense.
That I have done, as you cannot deny. I do not want to rule

here, Theora. I have my own wants and needs, and they are not those of a Makrala. But do not be deceived. The folk of Sherath are my concern, bred into my very bones. I am no docile dame to be sold like a mare for the breeding of princes. Do not think to use me as your tool or your weapon. I will not oppose you as long as you do not harm our father or our people. If you should do that, then be warned. I am not helpless."

Theora laughed. That knife-like laugh was becoming a thing to dread. "Play with the Guard. Learn to be a man-at arms, if you will. When I wear the Ring it will do you little good, sister mine. Powers more subtle and more potent will be mine—are already mine, indeed. I can shiver your paltry sword to atoms in your hand. No arrow can find me out as I stand within my field of power. I shall be invincible, whatever your delusions. Remember that."

Choria wanted a bath, but she wanted no gossiping maid servant to bring it. She flung on an old tunic and trousers and went down the backstairs, through the gardens, the orchards, to a stream that watered the row of houses along the street. It was enclosed within the walls of her father's landhold, free of intruders. There she stripped off her clothing and plunged into the cool water, ducking and snorting and trying to wash away the feeling her sister had given her.

A large opening, formed of cut stone, allowed the stream to flow from the holding upstream into that of the House. Another, downstream, did the same. She had always liked to lie at that opening, holding to the rough edge, letting the water sweep over her shoulders and neck, splash into her face. She did that now, feeling the grimy sensation flood away.

She realized, after a time, that she was hearing voices, conspiratorial voices, whose sibilances echoed through the stone channel, even above the rush of the water. She drew herself into the tunnel. Any conspiracy might well endanger her father, and she intended to investigate.

She pulled herself along the way by the rough comers of the stones, which had been cemented into place with a mix of mud and mortar. Keeping under the shelter of the farther lip of the opening, she found purchase and took a firm grip, easing her face near the rounded hole. The voices were very near.

The first word she heard caught her attention. "...danger!" it insisted. She raised her head to clear her ears of the water and listened with all her might.

"That is of no consequence. When the Makralo dies, whenever that may be, we shall be forced to deal with the Makra Theora. I fear that the day will come sooner rather than later. Not a pretty thought, eh, Sangrist?

"If we wait for the time to come before making plans, we will die at once, rather than in our own good time. But if we are organized, prepared, in touch with all those who support our position, then we may stand some chance of survival, even perhaps correcting the havoc she will raise in our land."

Choria knew that voice. She had fond memories of it I through her childhood. Bethor, Garrier's son. She had not known of his return from Algonath, although her father had told her that Bethor's Algon wife had died. So this was no conspiracy of traitors at all. These were concerned men, trying to prepare for an uncertain future. She hesitated, deciding ether to retreat or to make herself known.

The next words decided her. "If we could talk with the Makra Choria, it would be well. She is of the old stock, untainted. Her father has taught her well, my own father assures me of that. She can be the standard about which we rally, but that will be difficult. Her sister has her watched."

If that were true, she would imperil these men by her presence. She slipped back, a bit at a time, making no sound, until she was lying just inside the culvert. After a while, she let herself back down into the plunging water. It covered her completely. She thought that no one watching would be aware that she had gone inside the wet tunnel at all.

She came to the surface, shook her wet braid, and made for the bank, where a bit of coarse toweling waited with her clothing. She wrapped herself in that, took up the dirty things, and went toward the house. Though she held an impassive expression, her eyes were alert for any motion, any hint that she was, indeed, spied upon.

Beyond the line of berry vines, some yards from the stream, there was a stir of motion. A black-and-white bird flew from its covert, chacking irritably. She went on, undisturbed, knowing that she had, indeed, been watched. It was a thing she should have suspected. She would not again be surprised by her sister's spies.

CHAPTER FIVE

In time, the household settled a bit. Theora seemed to take her father's words to heart. She subdued her manners to a decent level. Everyone breathed sighs of relief, except Choria. She had had bitter experience as a child with Theora's ability to seem innocent and to behave diabolically at the same time. Her worst fear was for Orinath. He was not a man given to caution. He went about his city and his lands with only Garrier for a companion. Within his home, he would not allow the guard inside his door.

Until her sister came home, that had worried Choria. Now it terrified her. It would not take Theora long to find allies, no matter how well-off and content the people of Sherath might be. There were always those about a ruling house who had ambition greater than their wits.

She was also wary of Glagio. The tutor, with little to do now that Theora's education was complete, seemed ripe for mischief. She was, however, too cautious to approach her father about him. But Orinath was no fool. One summer morning Glagio was summoned to Orinath's study.

Choria learned about it from Garrier just in time to hurry to her listening post. She was worried that Orinath might do something to anger the man, to send him deeper into Theora's plots. She need not have been concerned. Orinath had handled men and women for more years than she had lived.

He greeted the tutor warmly. "My friend, I have had

no opportunity to speak privately with you since your return to my house. That is a shame, for I owe you much for your patience and care with my daughter. Do not think me unappreciative."

He drew the gratified tutor to a deep chair and offered him wine and fruit. When they were settled comfortably, the Makralo continued. "Your task being done, I have wondered how best to reward you. A generous pension is yours, of course, But I want to do something more. I have three suggestions for you to consider. Would you like stewardship of the North Steading? Or to be scribe and advisor to the merchantmen of Sherath? Or would you prefer to be my ambassador to Algonath? Any of these you may have for the asking."

"But—this is more than generous. I am honored, sir. I am overwhelmed. I had no idea you valued my poor efforts so highly."

"One cannot overvalue the work of the teacher of the Heir," said Orinath. Even the listening Choria could detect no sarcasm in his tone. "I had thought to choose a direction for you, but that would not be wise. No man can choose happily for another. Take the time to consider carefully, then let me know your decision."

Glagio was silent for a moment. Then he said, "There is no need for thought. I have spent my happiest hours at the North Steading, when the Family went there for midsummer. The farmers are solid folk, and I get on well with them. The families are civil, and Lord Gro and I have spent many pleasant hours playing at hart and huntsman on his big board, I choose the stewardship, with your kind permission."

Behind the chink in the marble, Choria was smiling. What an admirable man her father was! What a judge of men. Glagio was removed from the possibility of mischief, and instead of being bitter and angry, he was grateful and honored.

Theora, upon hearing the news, became a thunder-cloud, ready to spout lightning. Choria wondered what was said when she called her erstwhile tutor to her quarters. She did not dare try eavesdropping there, for the maids were always about. She did note that Glagio came away from that interview rather flushed and defensive. Theora did not emerge, even for the evening meal.

It was evident to Choria that some deep-laid plan had been set awry by the loss of her co-conspirator. She hoped that it would take years to set it right again. Yet she kept ears and eyes alert for any hint of conspiracy. She knew that their father's death was her sister's aim.

Time passed. Nothing unusual occurred. Choria slowly relaxed. Orinath settled into his routine, overseeing the agriculture, the road building, the maintenance of the city and the villages about it. Sherath was a land of quiet well-being, and most of that could be laid at the door of its Makralo.

Theora celebrated her eighteenth birthday amid celebrations and rejoicings. The common folk knew nothing of the darker side of their ruling family and would not have believed it if told. They put up banners of silk and linen, brought small gifts to the door of the House, cheered lustily when Theora went abroad into the city. She smiled mechanically, waved her flawless hand, scattered small coins from her window from time to time. But never did Choria see in her the faintest comprehension that these cheerful people were her responsibility, as well as her claim to power.

Winter came, with unusual cold and wind and inordinate amounts of snow. The public storehouses bulged with the grain and wool and dried meats that Orinath had ordered stored every year of his reign. The store had been needed very seldom and every spring it had been distributed to the very old, the infirm, and the feeble-minded. This year Orinath's foresight was a blessing, as the unprecedented winter settled over Sherath.

The cold weather went on and on and on. Time for the first thaw came and went without a hint of let-up. Ice covered ponds and streams; snow blanketed the streets and the fields and the forest to a depth half of a man's height. Supplies in private warehouses began running low. Those who had never before appeared before the Makralo to ask for help now began to come through the drifts, pleading for food to keep their families until spring might consent to come at last.

The storehouses began doling out their contents, thriftily but fairly.

"No one knows when this will end," the Measurers told those who came with bags and baskets. "We must make it last as long as possible. Otherwise we may starve later rather than sooner."

There was grumbling, of course. Not so much from the poor as from the well-to-do, who were not used to feeling slack in their bellies. Even those who shared the Makralo's table lost weight, for he refused to take more than the allotted share of his household. Theora raged, but Orinath stood firm,

"We can indulge ourselves when times are good and all our folk are fat," he told her. "Now we cannot waste anything. We cannot fill our own stomachs while others go hungry."

Choria was not happy with his words, but she understood their justice. Theora left the table and went to her room, where Choria was certain she had tidbits stored away against midnight hungers.

Before the storage houses were entirely empty, the weather began to ease. Winds became variable, switching southward for long enough to set the eaves dripping, then whipping from the north again for long enough to freeze the drips into sword-like icicles.

The day of the yearly spring celebration was long past

when the season finally arrived. One morning the sun broke through a high layer of thin cloud, beaming as if it really meant it. The wind shifted to the south and stayed there, bringing a thaw that threatened flooding downstream.

The streets of Sherath ran like brooks, leaking wet into stone cellars and sending the stream behind the Makralo's house rising almost to his doorstep.

Nobody minded the floods. Even the horses, standing almost fetlock-deep in water, seemed glad to exchange the discomfort of the past months for this new one. When the water had run away, grass leaped up with abandon, greening lawns and gardens, fields and wood paths.

Choria spent her seventeenth birthday quietly with her father and Garrier, riding through a forest whose leaves were just whipping open in the breeze.

She had relaxed a great deal in the past years. Theora had been difficult to live with, yet she had not done anything overt to disrupt the Family or her country. Perhaps, Choria thought, as she rode beside her father upon her tall mare, Theora had grown up, realized that her own way was not the law of the universe.

She should have realized that this was only wishful thinking.

CHAPTER SIX

The summer flowed past as peacefully as Sherath's summers usually did. Once gardens were producing again, crops greening in the fields along the river, people settled into their old contentment.

Yet Choria felt something niggling at her mind. A tide of unrest troubled her, and she felt a threat implicit in the very air, with its scents of flowers and fruits. It drove her to find a way to speak with Bethor and Sangrist. That was not as difficult as she had feared, for Garrier now determined that she was ready for sparring partners who were full-fledged warriors, instead of the young men-at-arms against whom she had trained thus far. When he asked what warrior she would like best, she smiled.

"Who could be better than your son, my friend? Bethor is much older than I. He could never be bothered with the small girl who wanted to tag after him. But now that I am becoming a warrior, too, perhaps he might change his mind. My father says that he is almost a rival of the skills you had at his age. Do you think he would agree?"

Garrier looked down at her. His gaze held something secret and pleased. "I shall trounce him if he does not!" he said with a grunt.

They spoke no more, for both knew they were spied upon, wherever they were, whatever they did. Yet Garrier knew, she felt, why it was that she had asked for his son. More than one conspiracy was aboil within the confines of the House. Only one was directed against the ruler of Sherath.

The next time she went into the drill room, Bethor waited for her in his linen practice clothing. He had been working and was already streaked with sweat as he saluted her and looked her over. "Do a spin turn with a block to the right," he told her.

She complied.

"Now drop to one knee, with upthrust and parry." She did that, too. Step by step, he put her through the complex maneuvers that his father had taught both of them, working through the heat of the day without pause for rest or food. Choria understood and approved. No battle will pause and wait while the combatants refresh themselves. When she was soaked and panting, and the sun was down in the west, he drew a long breath.

"You may dry off and lie on the bench while I talk with you. Don't sit—your muscles might cramp."

She knew that, but she said nothing. He brought her a draught of warmish water and handed her a hard biscuit to munch.

"You are trained as only Garrier can train a warrior. You have not much size, but you are strong and agile. What you lack in reach and weight, you make up in speed and inventiveness, I can help you there, I believe. If your opponent has no idea what you might do next, he cannot counter you. I have fought in Sparrv, when your father sent troops to aid their Elector, eight years ago. I have served in Algonath.

"What I learned there, I will teach to you." He was looking her from the comer of his eye, the glance carrying more than the mere weight of his words. "A younger child of a ruling house is in an unenviable position. You will need all the skill you can learn. I feel, after working with you, that you have the ability and the toughness to do what is necessary."

Choria knew that he understood why she had asked for him. Even as she puzzled over how to communicate with him directly, yet in an unsuspicious manner, he reached into a pouch beneath the bench. He pulled out a long belt of golden silk.

"Because it is usual for a Master to give a gift to his new pupil, I have this for you. It is beautiful enough for use anywhere, but it is strong and useful in war, as well." He caught the edges and. pulled across the weave. The fabric stretched into a thin, shimmering web as wide as her body and more.

"If you fall in battle, your comrades can spread your sash, and put you upon it, bearing you away between them. If you are wounded...."—he jerked lengthwise— "...the stuff can be hard and tight enough to tie off a severed artery. It can be used for tying prisoners, hanging bandits, blindfolding horses. Its uses are limited only by your own imagination. It is so durable that one single sash usually lasts a warrior his entire lifetime and is handed down to his children."

She took it from his hand and felt its gossamer texture. "It is a wonderful gift. I will treasure it always. But who makes such fine work? I know of no silk weaver in Sherath capable of it."

"There is one family in Algonath that does this weaving. My wife was a member of that family, and she wove this. The men tend the tiny creatures that spin the silk. The women unroll it and weave it into this magical stuff. You may be able to find the tiny symbols they weave into the cloth. That is the sign of their family's art." He sighed and rose. "Go now. Bathe and eat. Tomorrow will be harder. I will contend with you instead of putting you through your paces alone. Sleep well, little Makra."

Choria went up the many stairs to her modest room in the waiting-women's wing. The thing in her hands felt almost alive. The silk was warm to her touch.

More than one of Theora's maids found reason to do errands in her corridor as she went, but she held the sash with no more than moderate care and seemed not to notice the stares they directed toward it. A message had to be contained within it! She knew that. But nobody else must suspect.

She found her bath ready. Killa, who had been her maid before Theora's return, waited for her with warmed towels and fresh garments. That was suspicious in itself, but she laid aside the sash with her weapons, slid out of her clothing, and sank into the bath. It was good to have Killa's attentions again, Even though it was merely to distract her attention while someone went through the sash.

She didn't care. If the message were easy to find and to interpret, he would not have given it to her. It might, she felt, take her months or even years to decipher it. She looked forward to trying.

When she returned from the next room, where her meal waited, the sash seemed undisturbed. Yet when she touched it she knew that many hands had felt it over, searching for a hidden paper among its folds.

She laughed. Such obvious tricks were for those playing at deception. She was not playing. She and Bethor and Garrier were in deadly earnest. She waited until night, when the House sank into slumber, until even the prowling cats had given over their hunting. Then she went into the closet of her bedroom and kindled a spark for her candle. Closing the door, she took the sash between her hands, as Bethor had done. Holding it against the light, she could see tiny variations in the threads, making minute rough spots in the weave. That was the only thing she could find, though she searched all night.

It took her two weeks to find the code set into those tiny knots. Another month gave her the key. Then she had what she needed. She knew whom to call upon, if Theora suddenly came into power in a suspicious manner. So triumphant was she on the morning after learning the secret of the sash that she went down to the drill chamber and worked Bethor into a sweat of exertion and nervousness.

When they put up their weapons, he grinned at her. She knew he understood that his message had been received and comprehended. But he only said, "Well, if you go on like that, you must be teaching *me*! I have had bouts with men twice your size who wearied me less and gave me less ground for apprehension. If you intend to hire out as a mercenary in a few years, you are well prepared for it."

She laced up her sandal and smiled. "There would be worse ways of living. I cannot see remaining here, after my father is gone. And I am certain my sister would prefer that I go."

A hint of warning in his glance made her change the subject. It was wearisome to have every word pawed over by spies searching for a hint of conspiracy!

CHAPTER SEVEN

The use of weapons might be the most demanding of the things she studied, but it was not by any means the only one. No Makraitis had ever grown to adulthood without being given the finest education possible. Choria was no exception. Statecraft, accounting, languages of every nation bordering on her own—and even those at some distance but important to trade—were only a part of her lessons. Once she passed her childhood, she had no tutor.

"You know how to learn. Everything you will need is in the library. To know how to direct oneself is the most valuable lesson anyone can learn," her father had told her when she was fourteen. Though he made suggestions as to each new direction her studies might take, she was responsible for pacing herself, exploring researches among the leather tomes, writing minutely reasoned accounts of the results of her probings.

Yet the end of her education was drawing near. Theora was now nineteen. Her own eighteenth birthday was approaching. Another winter had passed, not so severe as the last but worse than usual in Sherath. The time of judgment was again at hand. This year, more than ever before, Choria felt uneasy. There had been a look in Theora's eyes that gave rise to apprehension.

The morning dawned bright but cool. Theora did not appear in the family breakfast room. Choria and her father ate together, without speaking. From time to time she

looked up to see him watching her, a quizzical expression
on his face. But still they said nothing. The things their
hearts wanted spoken were important, deeply felt. They
had no intention of letting an eavesdropper into the secrets
they held so closely. As they finished and stood, Orinath
turned to his younger daughter and put his arms around
her.

They stood so for a long moment, holding onto each
other, warm in that embrace. Choria was filled with a cold
foreboding. As soon as Orinath went to his room, she
moved to her own window and set into it a plant that Garrier had given her in advance of her birthday. Its appear-
ance in the window was a signal. Those who supported her
and her father would be at hand, if anything should go
amiss at the judging.

She dressed with care, not in the festival robes that
others were wearing, but in a set of leathers, the leggings
and tunic of which were overlaid with light mail. It had
been her father's gift. She put her sword in her sleeping
roll, with her bow and quiver and provisions she had pil-
fered from the kitchens. She slipped from the House early
and hid the roll amid the tumbles of stone about a ruined
house at the end of the street. Then she returned and stood
looking about her room. It felt like a last time. Something
told her that she would never return to it.

She wanted no escort to the Judgment Block. Unobtru-
sively, she worked her way near and stood up against it.
Nobody recognized her. She had not intended that they
should. She was in the place she had planned for herself,
whatever might come.

Orinath came in a blaze of glory, as his folk wanted.
Knowing how they enjoyed ritual and show, he had
dressed splendidly, as had his attendants. The herald, in
rich red brocade, raised his long horn and blew a blast,
bringing the crowd to attention.

Orinath climbed onto the Block. He looked about, then

raised his voice. "We have lived through another winter—one we would have thought severe another time. Some have not been pleased at their sharing from the common store. Yet we have all survived, save only those too old or too ill to live. Another spring greens the fields. A good crop is already in the ground. Let us rejoice, my friends, on this day of judging." He stood straight, hands at his sides, smiling and relaxed as he always was.

Anzil, the Master of the City, approached, bent his knee, and lifted the spear from its socket. With a roguish look, he touched it to his ruler's throat, bobbed his head, and returned the weapon to its place. Choria felt her heart slow again with relief. The Master had not been happy with his family's ration the past two winters.

One by one, those choosing to take part in the judging came and went. The spear was stainless. Choria began to relax. There were very few left, now. These were honest laborers and merchants, well-pleased to live in a city that was well found, under a ruler who kept the peace.

When she looked again, she saw a figure who brought a shiver to her spine. A slender woman stood at the end the line, her face half-hidden by a silken scarf.

It was a familiar shape, though Choria had never seen it before. Her aunt was much like her sister, so her father had said, and that dainty person stood with just Theora's arrogant grace. Could it be that Ellida had chosen to make the long journey from her own place for this judging?

As the figure stepped nearer to her turn, Choria felt herself freeze with dread. Her father had not seen, as yet—or did he just not show that he had seen? When the woman's hand touched the haft of the spear, he looked fully into her eyes. His smile was wry. Resigned.

The woman lifted the spear from its socket. "I have come far, on a mission of justice. You have tried to deny your first born the full extent of her heritage. You hid from her secrets and techniques that are necessary to those of our Family. Now I call you to account. I shall stand at her side as her adviser." The voice was icily sweet, cold as wind from the north.

Ellida thrust expertly (she was not like Theora in deriding the value of training in arms), and the keen head of the spear pierced Orinath's throat. Blood spurted, and he gave a gurgling groan and went slowly to his knees.

Choria leaped to his side, took his hand in both her own. With the last of his strength, he squeezed her fingers. Then he was gone.

There was turmoil about them. People withdrew from Ellida as if she were contaminated with some loathsome disease. She could not be struck down—the Law was adamant on that point. She looked about her, her eyes as cold as her voice had been. A ripple of fear ran across the crowd. Something about her demeanor told them that their days of peace and ease were past, dead with their Makralo. Now they would be ruled by a Makrala advised by this terrible woman. The escort moved to take up the body of their ruler. Choria released his hand and let them bear him away. Nobody paid heed to her. She sped down the street, retrieved her blade from her bundle, and hurried into the House by one of her secret ways.

She intercepted Ellida in the hallway, as the woman put aside her cloak and turned toward the stair. Choria stepped from the shadow of the statue standing there and looked into her aunt's eyes. "It was an ill day for you when Theora persuaded you to do this," she said, very quietly.

Ellida laughed. "Do you think to punish me? Foolish child! But we will cure you of such delusions, your sister and I. We will break you to our wills, be sure of that."

Choria did not reply. She braced her feet, raised her blade, and whaled off Ellida's head. Twin fountains of blood gushed forth, to spatter the pale statue with unbecoming red. Behind her there was a gasp of shock, an indrawn breath ready to shout for the Guard. But Choria was gone, out the door, down the street, out of the gates, and into the wood in which she had spent so much pleasant time with her father.

Garrier was ahead of her. Bethor and Sangrist were with him, together with some fifty men of the city, several young women, and a few striplings of no more than fifteen years. All were armed and clad for campaigning. And they were angry.

"Let us attack, now, while all is in turmoil!" one of the men shouted.

Garrier shook his head. "All is not in turmoil. Theora has planned this long and well. Those of the Guard whom she has turned to her side are ready for any such ill-timed attack. Ellida is with her—a formidable foe, that one. No, we would do well to rally in the forest, waiting for all who will join us. Then we will harry them, cut off the trade routes, take a toll of food supplies, though the farmers will gladly give it to us rather than to the Gatherers, if we ask it of them. They have long feared Theora, because she dislikes them and their work and does not know their value."

Choria cleared her throat. "Ellida is not with her." The others stared.

"She is dead. I cut off her head as she stood in the hallway of my father's House. She will not profit from her terrible deed. I saw to that."

"But the Law!" said Garrier, paling.

"Recall the wording of the Law, Garrier. It does not apply to those of the Family. Only to the folk of the city, the attendants, and servants of the Makralo. One cannot deprive a Makraitis of vengeance. Those who wrote the Law knew that. Yet I will be hunted and harried, make no mistake—that would have been true whatever happened, once they discovered that I would not serve their purposes."

Heads nodded. It was true. Choria was the antithesis of

43

her sister, a logical rallying point for any who opposed Theora's rule.

Mounts whinnied beyond them in the forest. Garrier said, "Then let us ride. We must hide well and quickly. Our watch will guide to us any who have good reason to find us." He looked about at the band of followers and sighed. "We are few. This was an ill day for Sherath. Worse will come, before all is done."

Mounting her mare, Choria knew that he spoke truly. She had heard her sister state her aims, long years ago. Now she was in a position to put them into effect. The folk of the city and the country about would feel the lash of her wrath before long.

They rode through the trees, found a path, and sped forward. Behind them, the city sparkled peacefully in the midday sunlight.

CHAPTER EIGHT

Choria lay in a clump of brambles, her limbs held motionless, her will straining to control the pounding of her heart, the laboring of her lungs. The clang of blade on blade, with an occasional grunt or shriek and the scuff of boots and clink of armor, filled the evening. She tried to rise, to join her people again, but she was too weak. She was half addled from a blow to the head, bleeding from many slighter wounds.

None were fatal, but she made no effort to stanch their flow. They could wait—there was no hot pulsing that would mean a severed artery. The Makraitis healed rapidly, and those minor cuts would tend themselves. They had done it many times in the past spring and early summer. She and her small band had given good account of themselves.

She listened. There was no more sound, except for the pounding of a drum. The recall! That meant that all her people were now dead or so sorely wounded as to be discounted.

She felt a pang of grief. They had been so faithful. So brave! Bethor—something inside her wept for him—Sangrist—Garrier. Tears started into her eyes, but she blinked them back.

Their courage had probably outweighed their good judgment. If they had remained at home, there might have come an opportunity to overthrow Theora without such a sacrifice this. Yet she knew, deep inside herself, that that was not true. They could only do what they had done, as could she. At the least, she had rid Sherath of Ellida.

She stared into the dusty brambles, hearing the last boot heels thump away into the distance. Now she could hear smothered moans, an occasional creak of metal as some sorely wounded man tried to ease his intolerable pain. Still she did not stir. Their enemies might have left someone on watch to see if she might not come to the aid of her men.

Only the approaching night had kept them from combing every inch of bramble thicket, every brush clump to find her. They surely thought her dead, but with any luck it would be tomorrow before they came to find her body. Only when it could not be found would they know certainly that she still lived.

Darkness grew deeper. Not even the chirpers spoke tonight. The battle had driven all the wild things deep into the forest rising to the west. Choria strained her ears. There was nothing except the small sounds of her wounded. Surely any watchers were now gone. She could go and give grace to those still lived.

She moved a leg cautiously. A score of cuts reopened and began to drip blood. She pushed herself up, quietly and with some difficulty. She was stiff, filled with pain, but she forced herself upright.

She steadied herself as her head spun. Then she kicked her way through the prickly mass toward the trampled area where they had fought.

"It is Choria," she called softly. "If you live, make some sound. I will come to you."

Almost at her feet, a voice grated, "Makra Choria! Give grace, I beg!"

She knelt and felt about for the form. Above it she made a sign with her forefinger and muttered a short incantation. When she was done, a bubble of dim light had formed; then by its glow she could see that this was Garrier.

He was covered with blood. His breastplate had been shorn away below the breastbone. He had been gut-thrust, a terrible wound, always fatal.

She dashed her wrist against her eyes. "Old friend, I give you grace," she said. But he reached to stop her hand before her tiny grace knife could find his throat.

"One moment. Your...father...charged me...to say this." He halted, gasping. His forehead ridged with effort. He drew a shallow breath, groaned, and began again. "The secret...arts...he could not teach you...were given...to your sister. He would have...taught you...if he could." The sunken eyes blinked hard, the knobbly throat moved again. "You remember...the hunting lodge?"

She nodded.

"Go there. Remove...the hearthstone. A...letter. Other...things. This last word...he bade me say. If you cannot prevent your sister...from her aims, kill her." The effort was too much. He took away his hand and lifted his chin to her knife.

"To the gods, Garrier," she choked, and the blade gave him grace. There was a quiet bubbling, then silence.

Another voice called softly to her. Another. Six times, the grace knife did its work. Six loved companions, including Sangrist, went to dwell with the gods of the Sheratha. She could not find Bethor's body in the darkness. She was grateful that she had not had to give him grace, too. That would have been more than her heart could bear.

She wondered for a moment if he might have been taken prisoner—but then she discarded the notion. Theora did not want prisoners. She wanted dead enemies.

Choria knew that she must escape, leaving no trace of her going. The forest was wide and wild. Few hunted

there, for the Sheratha were farmers by choice, not hunters. She and her father had savored their privacy in this
forest more than any hunting they had done.

The distant stars were giving a bit of light as Choria
went again to Garrier's side and laid her blade across his
ruined chest. She took his own keen weapon from his dead
hand and slipped it into her sheath. It would go forward
with her, taking with it, she hoped, something of his
strength and skill as she tried to wreak vengeance upon
those who had ruined his world.

She took from the others pouches of dried fruit and
meat, canisters of wine and water. They needed them no
longer, but she might want them badly, in days to come.
When she had what she needed, she pulled the twenty bodies straight in the blackness, moving by feel alone.

There had been many more, at the beginning of the ad-
venture. It grieved her to think of it as she closed their
staring eyes and drew the circle of peace upon each brow
in her own blood.

Those who came searching would know, then, that she
was certainly not dead. She was still abroad in Sherath.
They would come like hounds after a track, but she knew a
way—one of those forbidden arts her father had given
her—that would move her with no trace. Not far, for she
was too weak and drained to expend the energy for a great
crossing of space, but it would give her a distance between
herself and her enemies.

She stood in the cluster of her dead companions and
folded her hands together, though she had to use her left to
arrange the fingers of her right. Holding them waist-high,
she closed her eyes and concentrated upon a ferny spot beside a stream to the west, in the forest. A favorite fishing
spot, in the old days, where she and her father had caught
bright perch and slippery eels.

"Athero placetid canueritis," she whispered.

She was standing beside the stream, two hours along

on the way she must go. She had left no trace on the earth of her direction, for her foot had not trod the soil. It was a pity that she could not use this method for her entire journey but it drained her energies hugely. Even now she was feeling as if she might drop where she stood. She fell to her knees among the ferns and crawled to the burble of water that swirled slowly in the starlight.

It took some time to remove her leathers. It took longer to find and clean every cut worthy of the name. Those that had crusted with blood she let be, but those that seemed dirty she cut clean with her grace knife, packing them with crushed plantain.

Then she let herself lie flat among the cradling ferns. Dew formed on her skin and her hair, and the resumed leathers did little to keep her warm. She woke stiff and ill as dawn streaked the eastern sky. She forced herself to rise and to wash.

The chill of the water cleared her head. A frugal meal from the pouches gave her renewed energy. She waded the stream and set out toward the west, walking in the edge of the water to hide her tracks. When the stream looped northward, an hour later, the outriders of the great forest trees were all about her. She waded out onto dry ground and faced again to the west.

Recalling the way from many hunts with her father and Garrier, she found a narrow game trail running roughly in the direction she wanted. For two days she walked steadily, without hurrying but without stopping except to eat or to sleep, or when her fevered flesh would no longer move. At last, beside the path, she sighted a tremendous orhis tree that had grown around a standing gray stone until the megalith was almost completely contained within the huge gray trunk. She recognized it with grief and sadness.

"The stone of the Makraitis," she said, stepping up to lay her hand against the lichened rock. "When my father first showed this to me, did he suspect I might come again in such need to this place?" But there was no reply in the stone. Its virtue had long since departed, leached away by time and the demands of her ancestors.

Its position reminded her of the direction in which the lodge lay. She had to leave the path, pushing through ancient deadfall and debris that hid the secret trail. Before full darkness she saw the building loom before her, dark against the pale gray trunks of the orhis trees.

With relief, she went to the massive door and felt for the touch lock that her father had been the last to finger. Twice here. Three times on this point. Slip a finger around this gnarl. It should open.

It did.

CHAPTER NINE

There was no odor of mice or mildew inside that long-closed house. It held, instead, a watchful silence, as if some spirit stood guard there. The light staff leaned just inside the door, as always. Choria stood just within and concentrated her will upon it. Behind her, the forest was falling into chilly darkness. Before her, the staff kindled to a glow, answering her thought. The brilliance threw shadow across the deserted room, making it seem emptier of life than before.

They had always left their hideaway well stocked against a sudden whim to visit it. Though it had been years since that had been possible, there would still be dry wood in the bin beside the hearth. It would burn too quickly, but she kindled a blaze in the wide fireplace and warmed her hands for a moment. Then she began her exploration of the stones of the hearth. By the warm flicker, she began by digging with her fingers about the big stones at the front of the hearth's apron. In time, she took up the wood-spear they had used for managing large logs and dug with that.

The stones were solid, heavy. She had always thought them firmly mortared into place, but she found that the front rank was held by a sticky grit that only looked like mortar. It moved readily. She had the first of the flat stones heaved from its bed, then the second, then a third. Beneath the last, she could see the edge of a leather pouch lying beneath a fourth stone. When it was in her hand, she put the stones back as they had been and smoothed the false mortar between them again.

Reeling with fever and exhaustion, she set a pot out to remind her to fetch water from the spring. Only then did she sit down in the staghorn chair her great-grandsire had built with his own hands and take the pouch into her lap.

She found that she was trembling. For the first time, she realized the extent of her illness—the fever she had had for a long time had been subdued to her will. But she gathered herself again for the present and unfastened the wax seal closing the pouch. Inside was a long parchment, filled with her father's cobweb-fine script:

Makra Choria, Daughter

Greeting and Farewell:

If this be in your hand, then I am no more, and your sister sits upon the High Seat in Sherath. It is an ill day. Not because I begrudge the gods my death, but for my people and the city and the land I love and have tried to make prosperous.

I hope that Garrier may be with you, and others who cling to my ways. Yet I feel, with that sensing that is a part of our heritage, that you will be alone. On this assumption, I will proceed.

You know that I have not taught all the refinements and the safeguards of our heritage to your sister. Though Ellida gave her more than I wished for her to have, only I. as Heir, knew the most vital of the arts of our Family. My brother, knowing what he intended to do, spent his last year teaching me the things that I had to know as Makralo. I have written for you all the things that you might need to know, if the position comes to you. I also have written the techniques my brother devised for controlling, or even removing, the power from a Makraitis. I could, before his death, have used those techniques and saved his life, for at that time I was not Makralo. I wish that he had taken that choice, but he did not. You, being Makra, can use them, if you have the opportunity.

All these matters I give to you, being dead and above the Law. Do not, however, think that this will give you an easy victory over Theora. She has in her the strong convictions and the stronger talents that belong to any Makraitis.

Remember this: she does not think herself wrong. She is not deliberately trying to become a villain; that is a pernicious thing about our kind—we can convince ourselves that what we desire is, beyond doubt, the best thing for everyone. It is possible that, even now, she could be saved from herself. I hope it deeply.

Within this pouch are the writings. You must memorize them, then destroy them. Only if you find yourself again in such a situation as I do now, leaving your child needing guidance, may you commit them to paper once more.

Within this house you will find all that you need to perfect your skill in the arts described herein. There are vessels of strange properties and mechanisms of unusual design. These will help you in your purposes. When you are done with them, destroy them also.

Go carefully, Choria. Know that if there be thought beyond death, mine will be with you, as is my love, always.

I command you, my last such as your father: either stop your sister or kill her. Save my country from the destruction she will visit upon it.

Leave no scrap of this letter unburnt.

Orinath,
Makralo of Sherath

Choria found herself burning with fever, desperately thirsty. Water—she must have it now. The words of the letter swam in her mind, and she knew she must read it again I before burning it. Now she must go to the brook, while she still had the strength.

Staggering up from her chair, she laid the letter and the pouch upon a table and caught up the pot. It seemed a long way to the spring. It was longer, yet, returning. She drank deeply, nibbled dry fruit. It threatened to choke her. She was too ill. Only her will had brought her here. Now her overburdened body demanded full payment for its efforts. She stacked more wood on the fire, rolled herself in a bearskin on the huge couch before it. Her eyes closed. She gave herself over to her desperate weariness.

She never knew exactly how long she lingered in the embrace of the fever. It might have been days or weeks. When she opened her eyes with a clear mind, it was to see chinks of sunlight streaking the low ceiling of the room. Ash, long dead, powdered the hearth. The pouch lay as she had left it, with the letter. The pot of water was almost empty, and she knew she must have drunk, even in her stupor.

She rose, feeling terribly light in the bone, and knelt to kindle a fresh fire. A trip to the spring provided water in which to boil dried meat. Only broth would sit upon her queasy stomach now, she knew. She must eat, to gain strength. There was much to do!

With broth and a bit of stewed fruit inside her, she felt more like herself. By evening she was clear enough to re-read the letter and to tackle the directions in the pouch. Within three days, she had memorized the intricate procedures and incantations faultlessly. In less than another week she had used those "vessels of strange properties" hidden beneath the lodge, and held within herself potent abilities that her father had denied to Theora. It took another week to bring her body to the level her mind had already reached. Then she looked eastward again.

Her journey to the lodge had been slowed by wounds and illness; her return to Sherath was not. She did not stop to hunt, but brought down occasional hares with her bow. She had no time for squeamishness. Any chance encounter with a forester would warn her sister that she was coming.

She must move like the wind, without squandering any of her hard-won strength in the doing. But once she came into the forest beside Sherath, she came to a halt.

CHAPTER TEN

Beside the same stream to which she had fled from the battleground, though at a different part, she began preparing for her lone battle. She formed a pattern of white pebbles from the streambed. Within it she sketched a face, using the stem of a reed for an instrument. It was not her face. That was a long oval, framed in red-gold hair.

This was a stolid, square face, undistinguishable from a hundred others. She dripped water upon it, forming pockmarks. She laid half-rotted waterweed about it for lank black hair. Then she stood and spoke.

"Ilisis adenuate. Ilisis adenoarat. Ilisis adenont."

When she stooped above the pool, she saw that unfamiliar face staring back at her. Satisfied, she removed her mail, her padded undergarments, and put them into a bag she had brought from the lodge. From it she took a peasant's smock of raw fiber, a pair of sandals, and a broad hat, part of the store at the lodge. Once she was dressed and had looked again into the pool, she felt that her own father would pass her by, unaware of her identity.

She put her weapons into the sort of pack that peasant girls used and made her way south, toward the road running up through the farmlands and down to Esselat on the southern sea. She came up to Sherath among herds and carts loaded with produce for the city. There were others who walked alone, going to seek work there. They were mostly young, threadbare, and shy. She patterned her behavior on theirs.

Just outside the city she found excuse to drop away from the road and hide the bag with her leathers, but she kept the one with her sword. Then she rejoined the two young women she had come to know. They went together through the tall gateway.

Though the girls had chattered like magpies on the road, they were suddenly shy at the moment of parting.

"Come with us," they begged Choria. "We will find work as seamstresses together."

"I know nothing but farm work," she replied. "I hope to find employment in some stable. Perhaps even at the High House. But I will look for you, in time, and see how you fare."

She watched them out of sight, trudging toward the Hall of Servants. Her way was hers alone, and she waited until the street was empty of anyone interested in her before taking it.

She went into the old part of town, which edged one of the streets that ran along three sides of the House of her fathers. The ancient parts of the House were, indeed, a part of a ruined complex to which she made her way. She knew every cranny and rat hole there. Passages existed beneath the very noses of the Guard. She had come and gone, as a child, without anyone being the wiser. Once she was old enough to know that Theora had her watched, she had gone there no more, wanting to keep her secrets.

It was almost too easy. No one questioned her or even glanced her way. Guardsmen she had known all her life passed without glancing at her. She blessed her impulse to add pock-marks to her new face. That had been an inspiration, for any sign of the pox was repellent, even to the lustiest Guardsman.

She found herself, at last, before the ruined house that had been her goal. The hour was late. Most had taken themselves off to their homes for the evening. On the wall of the High House, she could see two Guardsmen stalking along, their shadows gigantic upon the faces of the houses looking westward. She was already in shadow. When they turned, she ducked into the sagging doorway, squeezing past the hinge-sprung door.

Dust, mildew—the acrid tang of rats took her back to her childhood. Yet the house seemed no more tumbledown than it had years before. Not even a ceiling had fallen.

She was able to pick her way among rotted bits of furniture toward the rear, where she went into the sculleries and down a stone stair into the cellars. Once the still-solid door closed behind her, she called forth her bubble of light. That kept her from breaking her neck on the slimy stone steps.

The cellars were cut into the stone of the city's bedrock. At the back of the farthest compartment, there was a wide crack in the stone, caused by some long-forgotten stress or shift. It was large enough for a thin person to work into, if she were not afraid of tight places—and if she had the nerve to face whatever tenants might have taken up residence in the dark depths.

Choria had traveled that way before, forcing herself through the narrow way. She hated close confinement, as well as spiders. She shuddered at the memory of the thick webs she had found there, and the chitterings of the vermin before and behind her.

But this was the way to Theora. Here she must go, once more.

She unslung her pack and took her blade from its wrappings. Then she went forward, holding it ready to fend off anything that threatened her, and dragging the pack behind her. She had no guarantee that Theora had not found this entryway and set a guard here, since last she had known it. Fighting her way through the dust-filled crack, she thought of her sister. How little real contact they had had, even as small children. It was difficult to judge, at

58

this distance, how much of her sister's problem might be blamed on the constant watchfulness of her parents and nurses.

Could it have been the unloving vigil kept constantly upon her that had turned Theora more deeply into her power-hungry ways? How was it possible for an infant to hold so much evil within herself that her own mother had been driven to murder her? And yet, recalling every moment spent in her sister's company, Choria had to admit that something within the girl chilled her to the bone.

She came to herself with a jerk. Something had ducked into a crevice ahead of her, stirring a small swirl of dust as it came to rest. As she came near, her light-bubble floating ahead of her, bright eyes stared at her from the niche.

A tumble of stone, around which she had to edge, marked the halfway point of her journey. She knew that she was now beneath the House itself. She shivered with sudden chill—Theora. She had always been able to feel her presence in that way, even at some distance. She wondered, suddenly, if Theora had that sensing of her—it seemed probable. But she was committed. Things must happen as they would.

As she worked forward in the dimness, she wondered if her doubt, there in the passage, might be some kind of trap by her sister. For her, or perhaps for any who might venture there. She shivered again and forged ahead. It wasn't far to the opening into the stables.

She saw light. Dim and dusty still, but it marked the end of this part of her way. She cat-footed toward the hidden entry. Peering through the loose boards into a forgotten comer of the stable complex, she saw no movement, heard no sound. Strange. There should be many horses there—or had the Guard taken them for an exercise or a foray? Not a stamp, not a whiffle or snort came to her ears.

It seemed too apt, too easy. Yet here she was, and she did not intend to go back or to hesitate. She slipped between the sagging boards and settled her pack again upon her shoulders, grateful that she had left the bulk of her equipment hidden in the fields.

She rose slightly to glance over the edge of the stall. There was no motion in the long building. Yet the ring of iron on iron told her that the smith was busy with some of the horses out in the big paddock.

There were many ways to get into the house from the stables. She chose the safest and shortest route, up the maids' stair, through the servants' quarters. This put her at a small door leading into the long gallery overlooking the dining hall. The gallery was empty. Once more, her instinct warned her that this was altogether too easy. Theora was too talented, in her bitter way, too skilled at self protection to allow anyone to gain such effortless access to her House.

Choria stifled that internal warning. So be it. At the least, she had not been forced to fight her way into her sister's dwelling. She was here, with her own energies undepleted. Yet, inside her, her father's warning seemed to echo. Theora was near, too—every sense hummed with her presence.

Choria stepped to the spindled railing and looked down into the hall. Theora sat in the High Seat at the end of that long chamber. Even at this distance, she looked smug.

"Come down, little sister. Join me in the hall of our ancestors. You ran away too soon—I intended to entertain you here long ago. With our aunt in attendance. But better late than never, as the peasants say." Her voice was honeyed, with a tang of acid.

She hadn't really thought that she might surprise her sister. A woman of her talents cannot be surprised on her own ground, Choria knew all too well. Her only chance lay in surprise on another level—or physical attack.

Now that the time was at hand, Choria found herself

completely calm. She left her small pack in the gallery, but her blade was in her belt as she moved down the stair. She would not try it against Theora, but any of her henchmen who were about might well feel its edge.

"You come armed into the presence of the holder of the High Seat?" asked Theora.

Choria stepped onto the stone-flagged floor of the hall. "Those of the Blood may do so," she said civilly. "If you recall your education, sister. This is within my right as a Makra of the Makraitis."

Theora's eyes narrowed, the violet irises gleaming between pale lids. Her face, oval like her sister's, flushed. "True. But subject to change. As all things are."

"Including the principles of our fathers? The responsibility for our people's welfare? The care for those dependent upon us, and the care and concern for our neighbors?" Choria's voice was light and steady. "Have those things changed, Theora?"

Theora's laugh was genuinely amused. "Especially those things," She chuckled again. "I find it hard to believe that those whose blood runs in my own veins propounded such counterproductive policies. Power is power, small sister. It exists in order to exist in order to exist. Those who hold it desire more, always. It is a rule of nature. The Makraitis deceived themselves for generations, pretending that their power was different from the other sorts. But it is all the same. And now it has come into the hands of one who knows how to use it."

Her eyes flashed violet fire. "You noted, I am sure, that the stables were all but empty when you came through your rat-run in the ruins. Most of the beasts are gone, with their riders, on a sortie against Algonath. Ten thousand foot soldiers marched eastward with them. We shall rule in Algon before winter."

Choria felt sick. Her people were not good warriors, though they were fine farmers and herdsmen and foresters.

And Algonath was a neighbor and a friend.

"Not as volunteers, I presume," she said, still in that light, dry voice.

This time Theora's laugh rang loudly through the room. "Oh, come now! Even you cannot think that the clods I rule would ever volunteer for war! They were dragged from their homes, fitted with neckbands of my own design, and drilled until they managed not to trip one another. Those metal bands—you would find them interesting. I have keyed them to my Ring. Our fathers' Ring. The Ring of the Makraitis. Any deviation from their set duties disturbs the power-flux. They attract my attention, and I send them death in painful forms. Most edifying for their fellows. Some had thought to desert." She laughed again.

Choria heard her out. She felt sick, but she drew on the energies she had so painstakingly built up for herself. She formed a bubble of light above her head that grew in intensity and size. It darted toward Theora, who deflected it without effort. Yet the bubble did not wink out. It shrank and settled near the ceiling.

Something settled about Choria's windpipe, squeezing, choking. She raised her hands to pull it away, but there was nothing for her fingers to catch. She felt her eyes bulging, panic touching her heart, yet she understood what was happening.

She called upon all her ability for calm. She stopped struggling for breath. The pressure eased. She closed her eyes and pictured a vise closing upon her sister's torso, squeezing her narrow waist, pinching it into two parts.

The pressure vanished. She heard a grunt of pain from her sister.

While Theora struggled to remove this temporary inconvenience. Choria fixed her gaze upon the bowl of water set for cleaning hands at table. With a part of her mind, she set her will upon the bedrock of the city, through which she had come into the House.

"Tremble!" she commanded the water.

"Shake to your foundations!" she whispered to the stone.

Theora fought free of the squeezing and drew a gasping breath, "You are...stronger...than I supposed," she choked. "I believe that our father did not narrowly observe the Law."

She hissed between her teeth. Mist rose about her chair, the tendrils weaving across the space between them toward Choria. At first gray-blue, they changed hue to a sickly green. A stench filled the room. Where the first veils of mist touched Choria felt her skin grow cold, her muscles numb.

She ignored her own discomfort, however. She was bending all her effort upon the bowl of water. Her borrowed face crinkled with concentration as she willed wavelets to rise on the surface of the water contained in the vessel. Some part of her felt dust begin sifting down in the crack below the House.

Theora's face was hidden behind the mist, when she glanced up from the bowl. When she looked down again even the bowl was hidden by the curdling green vapors. Still, she could see it in her mind. She pushed it into waves. In her vision the vapors thinned, and Choria could see ripples moving uneasily back and forth across the water in the bowl. Now, plainly, there was a groaning of stone upon stone.

It was clear that Theora heard it, too. Her violet eyes were flashing urgently, and Choria felt their stare.

"What have you done?" Theora gasped, as the flagstones of the floor heaved and cracked beneath her. She came tumbling down from the High Seat, which broke into pieces.

"I am troubling the land," said Choria, though with effort. The remnants of the mist had wrapped her around.

She could barely move her lips. Only her will was unaffected by the poisonous fog.

Then the buckling of the floor upset her, in her turn. She fell, rolling beneath the veils of the mist. Sensation returned to her body, but she ignored it, holding her will firmly upon her purpose.

"Tremble, waters! Shake, lands! Shudder, stones! Set the city dancing! Topple the High House, which has been misused by its tenant!" She uttered no sound, but those commands flowed out of her. Though the bowl of water was spilled onto the floor, the tumult increased. Something fell, crashing—she thought it was a balcony.

Theora cried out, as she rolled through the mist, which cleared before her. She glared down at Choria, shrilling, "You are destroying my House, the seat of our ancestors! Be done, traitress, before you bring down everything!"

"I intend to do that," said Choria. She rose, at last, to face her sister. "Listen!"

Groaning and cracking, stone whining against stone and metal against wood, the great House heaved and listed. The gallery at the end of the hall fell onto the flagstones, its carved spindles flying like arrows. One caught Theora against the back of her head. She dropped in a heap.

Choria seized her sister, heaved her across her back, and made for the doorway leading into the entry. Behind her, she could hear the House dying amid crashings and roars and grindings.

She sped into the courtyard. It was thick with dust. Bodies pushed past her and hands tugged at her clothing, but it was too dim to see or to be seen. None hindered her as she took her unconscious sister out of the sprung gateway and into the street. Even there, houses danced mad pavanes, and their tenants were scampering about, out of their wits with terror.

Moving as fast as possible, burdened as she was, she

went toward the southern gate. Voices cried questions and bewildered answers all about her as she went. One of these exchanges caught her attention.

"What of the Makrala?"

"Pray the bitch is dead!"

She sighed with relief. She had made no error, then, in bringing down the House of her fathers.

The gate, when she reached it, was unguarded. She knew that the guards had gone to see to their own families, as they should have done. She went through it, taking the road only as far as the long meadow lying to the east of the city.

To the east, in the mountains, lay Algonath. There was the army of Sherath, soon to be called home by whatever power seized the rulership of Sherath. There was no doubt in her mind that Algonath was disturbed, angry, but she intended to go there. Some force inside her told her that her fortune lay in that direction.

Theora stirred on her shoulder and groaned. Choria tightened her grip and hurried into the cover of the hedges. She dumped her burden onto the damp ground and tied her hands together with strips of her own petticoat.

Then, as the girl struggled to regain consciousness, Choria did the thing she had learned from her father's instructions at the lodge. She chained the powers that were inborn in the Makraitis. It was, she felt, better than killing, when all was accounted for.

The spell was long and wearing. In her distressed state she thought she would faint before it was done, yet she intoned the thing to its end. And then she turned it against herself and her own powers. It took the last of her energy, and she felt her own likeness return as it ebbed.

Theora was staring up at her, now in her own face. "What have you done?" she shrieked. "Madwoman!"

Choria smiled down at her. "We are only two women now, sister. Cast adrift into the world, homeless, fatherless. You will not dare return, powerless, to Sherath. The people would tear you apart. I will not go there again, with or without power, until I feel that I can make some amends for your faults. We two are commoners, now. No power. No high place of birth. No wealth. I shall go eastward. Perhaps there is something I can do toward healing some of the wounds your ambition has caused in Algonath. I felt a compulsion, as I set aside my Gift. I feel it even now. Something calls me eastward...." She frowned, concentrating. Then she shook her head and sighed.

The violet eyes were filled with disbelief. "No one willingly gives up power! Surely you have kept your own. I can feel only emptiness where my own strengths lay, but even you could not be so foolish as to relinquish yours."

"I will not argue with you," replied Choria. "I am going upon my way. Let me cut loose your hands. You can go upon yours."

When Theora stood, free, on the grass of the meadow, Choria set out eastward, after resuming her own garments, retrieved from her hidden bundle. She followed the cattle paths through the meadows. Before reaching the next hedgerow, she heard the scuffle of feet behind her.

She sighed. In solving one problem, she had burdened herself with another. Even powerless, Theora would be a handful.

She smiled, rather grimly.

"Come, sister. Take my hand. We have a long way to go."

CHAPTER ELEVEN

Summer had dwindled to fall. Long miles lay behind Choria when at last she found a place in which to rest over the winter. It was not, needless to say, a place that pleased her sister.

The track of destruction they had followed led straight toward Algonath. Along it there was nothing—no town left tenanted, no farm left productive, no orchard left unstripped of its fruit. Choria had veered off to the north, taking a little-known track her father had shown her years before. It was no easy way, scrambling upward through the foothills, along the deep ravines beside streams that carried away the waters from the winter's snows.

There were few dwellers in this difficult country. Huntsmen, foresters, a very few tiny farms set into pockets of rich soil cupped in stone outcrops. As the clouds of winter banked along the northern sky, the two sisters came upon such a croft, snug in a small valley laid like a porch along the side of a mountain. Even as they moved to its cattle-hide door, the wind began bringing big flakes of white down upon their heads.

"We beg shelter!" Choria called. "Is anyone in the house?" Theora shivered beside her, huddling against her leather cloak.

"We will freeze," she complained through chattering teeth. "You have done what you intended—brought me to my death. Father would be proud of you!"

Choria had learned weeks before to shut her ears to Theora's complaints. It had taken less time by far to teach her sister that she must pull her own weight or be left behind. That much had been accomplished, if nothing else, but to make her hold her tongue was a more difficult matter.

There had been no sound from the hut, which was less real house than a pile of artfully arranged stones chinked with mud and grass. Now the cowhide was thrust aside, and a skinny arm came into view.

"Who be ye?" came a grudging whisper. "No demon of the snow will I let into my holt. No thief or outlaw will I harbor. Never think that ye can overpower this old dame. I've powers to make your hair stand on end, your skin to crinkle with terror."

Choria laughed softly. "Powers we do not fear, old woman. Snow we do. And we are harmless to those who mean us no harm. Two young women stand at your door. We flee only from the storm."

The cowhide was pushed even farther back. "Then come in, But mind—I keep me floor, be it earthen or no. Clean your feet and mind your manners."

Theora pushed past her sister into the hut. Choria follow more slowly, lowering the hide door into place with some relief. When it was tied at sides and bottom, the wind was fairly well stopped out of the cramped interior of the room.

She turned to see the old dame watching her intently. She had expected to find one like the charlatans that preyed on the ignorant in Sherath, pretending to powers they only guessed at. This woman was not, it was instantly apparent, one of that sort.

"Oho! And what sends Makraitis out into the world on their own? I've heard no word from the lowlands for over a year—things must have turned and shaken for the two Makra to be wanting shelter from such as I am."

Choria went forward the short distance between them and stood looking into the dim gray eyes turned so sharply upon her. She stood for a long space, eye to eye. Then the woman nodded, slowly, three times. "Ahhh. So. And he is gone, then, to his fathers." A tear leaked from the corner of a wrinkled eyelid and slid down a crumpled cheek. She turned to look searchingly at Theora. "And this is the parricide, then?"

Choria saw a scathing reply rise to Theora's lips—and freeze there. Stiffly as any doll, she took three steps forward until she was directly before the old woman. Choria wanted to laugh. In just this way had her sister compelled people, when she had the power. It was just that she learn exactly how it felt to be so manipulated.

"Makrala! So you abused your position. Angered those you were supposed to protect. Tried to kill your sister after having your father murdered. A pretty thing you are! And now you come to my door in the teeth of a snowstorm, wanting to be coddled and cosseted. Well, it will be far different, Makrala, You will dance to my tune, believe it."

She turned her dim gaze again toward Choria. "And...," she began, but the girl interrupted her.

"I am a hunter of some skill. I will work at anything that needs doing. But I will not be compelled so. Indeed, I think it might be true that you cannot compel me so, even though I voluntarily gave up my claim to the powers of my kind. Do not think to have two puppets on your string."

The woman cackled shrilly. "A true Makraitis! Orinath's get, beyond all doubt. Welcome, Makra, to the house of Willowill. In the old days, I knew your father. He came to me, once or twice, for advice, when I had not yet come to the high places to get away from fools. Not that he was a fool, you understand. But many were. Many were."

"And still are," answered Choria. "Yet they did not deserve what she gave them." She nodded toward Theora, who was struggling to open her mouth, to move, but could do neither.

Willowill chuckled. "I saw into you, just now. You are no weakling, power or none. You made your body serve your will, your will serve your purposes. An unusual thing for anyone, but even more for a Makraitis. While she relied upon that ring! It makes a great difference—but why yammer about it? She is my puppet. You are not. Will you be my guest—and perhaps, in time, my friend?"

"Perhaps. I have learned not to trust quickly—or even at all—in my short life," Choria said.

"Then we shall have our supper served up in style," said Willowill. "Woman, there are bowls in the cabinet over there. Take three and fill them with stew." She concentrated upon Theora, as she went stiffly and protestingly about doing just that.

Choria, watching, observed, "It seems more trouble than it is worth, to me."

"In most cases that is true. But I am a wicked old woman. I like to see people squirm, particularly if they deserve to. Your sister most richly deserves to. And...."—Her tone was less acerbic—"...it is educational. You have come to the right person, perhaps accidentally, perhaps not. I can make a sensible person of your Makrala, given time."

CHAPTER TWELVE

Angry though she might be at her involuntary servitude, Theora had to be grateful for the shelter of Willowill's house that night. Outside, the wind flung snow against the rough stones, whistled through the crevices in the walls, gusted down the rude chimney to scatter sparks about the small chamber. It was no night for sleeping beneath the sky.

Choria had carried in a huge pile of wood and placed it, as directed, in a nook at the back of the chamber that had been hollowed out of the solid stone of the mountainside. Willowill had become almost affable. Having two to help her, as well as having someone to talk with, put her into a better mood as the evening wore on.

They sat before the fire, listening to the crackle of the fir wood and the howling of the wind, stretching their feet to the warmth. Rude as the hut might be, it felt palatial to Choria after the many nights of sleeping in fields or in the wrecks of abandoned sheds and barns.

Theora had been released from her puppet-like state and sat glowering into the flames. Choria knew that her sister longed to lash out at both of her companions, both physically and verbally. Only the fear of being thrust out into that storm held her silent. It had taken several such incidents to prove to Theora that Choria would, indeed, remove her bodily when her tongue became too hurtful. She had spent more than one night barred out of a shed, sleeping on the grass. It was a lesson well learned, however, and she said nothing as Choria looked across the warm-lit arc of firelight at Willowill.

"My father used to visit you for advice? It says good things about your wisdom—and your discretion. Can you tell me what it was that he asked you?"

Willowill was chewing on a leaf of some sort. It turned her lips a poisonous green, and when she opened her mouth her tongue was also green. But her voice had lost a little of its sharpness when she replied.

"He's dead, now. The country, I can see in you both, is at sixes and sevens. Who is to be hurt? She...."—she nodded toward Theora—"...needs to be shaken to her roots, even yet. So I will tell you the thing that your father asked of me. I pitied him then, and I pity him now. It was a bitter thing for a parent to be compelled to ask."

Choria glanced toward Theora. Though the Makrala's position had not changed, there was a tension about her stillness that told her sister she was paying close attention to the conversation.

"It was not the first time I had met with Orinath, Makralo. After the birth of his first child, he had called me to attend his wife. Doubtless, you know the source of her trouble at that time. I was famed, in certain circles, for my herb craft, and I was able to soothe her with infusions. While I sat by her side, she told me things that she did not confide to her husband for a long time. She had felt the warping of her child's Gift, even in the womb. She was powerless to stop it, powerless to alter it." Willowill spat a green stream into the fire, which sputtered purple sparks for a moment afterward.

"I knew, even before he did, that the Heir was flawed," she said.

Theora raised her head, her violet eyes sparking in the firelight. "Flawed?" she growled. "Flawed, do you say? Say rather, the Heir had regained the sense her kind had lost."

Willowill spat again, and a long purple flame rose in the fireplace. "Badly flawed. But I said nothing, for the mother swore me to silence, and to comfort her I made my oath. And she died, poor lady, giving birth to her second child. Not before telling her husband what she feared for her first."

"My father told me all that," Choria said. She put out her foot and pushed back the end of a burning chunk of wood. The fire burned more brightly. "What did he ask of you? That is the thing I want to know."

"How to straighten a warped mind and heart. How to repair a Gift gone wrong. Without killing the child, if possible. But, failing that, how to kill the child painlessly and in a way the Law would never suspect."

Choria nodded. "That is what I thought it might be. And what did you tell him?"

"To circumvent the Law in any way he could devise. To keep from the Heir all that he could of the powers of her kind and to make certain that his second child had a chance to learn things that tradition forbade her knowing."

"So it was you...who are the ultimate source of my ability to remove Theora from the High Seat. Interesting. He did what you advised, you know. He left instructions for me for a time when he would no longer be able to rule or to teach. Our country has reason to be grateful to you. She was sending our good farmers, our skilled woodsmen to waste their blood in an unjust attempt to conquer our neighbor."

Willowill cackled. "Do you think that chance brought you to my door in a storm that demanded shelter? Never think it!"

"You brought us here?" That was Theora, her voice quiet and venomous.

Willowill looked sharply at the girl. "Not I. The Will that gave me what meager power I possess. The Will that provided the Makraitis with the abilities that make good rulers. The Will that was thwarted by something in your heritage. Nothing happens by chance, child. No matter how strange and unlikely it may seem, all conforms to a pattern too large for our limited vision to make out. You are here for a purpose, as is your sister. I suspect what it may be. You will know, as well, before long."

There was a howl of wind in the chimney. Sparks flew into their faces, mixed with smoke. Choria rose to put the fire into order again, but the old woman shook her head.

"Bank the fire, child. It is time we were abed. Tomorrow the wind will die away, but the snow will be high. There will be work to do for all of us." She grinned wickedly at Theora. "Willing or not."

Choria pushed the log ends together and covered them deeply with ashes. When she was done, she turned to the old woman. "And where do we sleep? Here before the fire?"

Willowill rose creakily. "My house is larger than it looks. Come with me—around the chest, here—and into my passageway."

Sure enough, Choria found that the house was formed not only of the stone walls, but of natural passages and chambers in the rock of the mountain against which it had been built.

"You may choose to sleep apart or together. There is room for many, back here. But it is cold. You'd best share warmth. The stone has been chilled for ages and is impossible to warm." She gestured into a modest-sized room that was rounded on one side and squared on three more. "This should do you quite well."

She pottered away down the winding passage, leaving Choria and Theora staring about in the flicker of a torch. The room wasn't icy at all. Yet there was a persistent chill that did not invite one to remove clothing or to dawdle about getting into the bed, which was a pile of fragrant fir tips covered over with a heavy homespun cloth. A pile of beautifully dressed furs lay at hand for covering.

Without conversation, Choria and Theora lay on the bed and pulled furs about their ears. Their backs touched, in a grateful point of warmth. It was, Choria thought sadly, the only warmth there had ever been between them.

CHAPTER THIRTEEN

It was a winter even more fierce and long-lasting than those that had gone before it. No matter how much wood the women scrounged from the snow-laden forest and stored in their cavernous deeps, it was always soon consumed. Choria and Theora found themselves dreading their foraging expeditions more and more, as time dragged past.

Willowill was sometimes lively company. Perhaps one evening out of five found her ready to sit before the fire, after their thrifty meal of batter-cakes or dried meat, spinning tales of long lost days when she lived in Sherath. But the other evenings were far different. She would glower at them over her bowl of mashed batter-cake mixed with water (her teeth were not spaced well for chewing), and as soon as she was done she would mutter her way off to her own chamber, leaving her unwilling guests to their own devices.

Food was not so plentiful as it might have been. Willowill had stocked her larder as well as possible, but she had expected only herself to winter over in her house. Scrimp as they might, the stock of meal and grain, of dried meat and fruit, dwindled. And there was no thought of going on with the journey the sisters had begun. Snow packed the passes, loomed in dangerous lips over the small valley, and slid in thunderous avalanches down the heights above Willowill's house, which was set close against an overhanging cliff. Those slides went sailing down, missing the front door by scant yards, to pile in billowing drifts at the bottom of the cleft beyond the dooryard.

A time came when there had to be more food. A short thaw had left the ground too dangerous for moving. A new freeze, with snow, firmed it again, and Choria put on her leathers, a huge cloak of fur that Willowill dug from some hidden storage, and the boots she had worn away from her home.

She did not ask Theora to join her. The task would be difficult enough, if she could find game at all. Her sister would be a hindrance, not a help.

To her surprise, when she was ready to open the door, Willowill joined her there. The old woman was wrapped to her eyes in furs, but she moved with alacrity. She hopped into the snow like some ill-shaped bird, and Choria hid a chuckle as she followed the crone toward the path leading downslope into the wood that furred the mountainside.

"The snow hares den in the wood. I am not spry enough to catch them, as I used to do, but with you to help me, we should return with meat, if nothing else," the woman croaked, pouncing onto a hummock beside their path and burrowing into it with both hands.

The snow flew out in a rooster tail as she dug. Choria moved to stand on the other side of the mound, waiting to see if any small beast might fly out into her hands. Only a stump came into view. Willowill snorted, put both hands to her back, and stood creakily.

"Eyes are not what they were," she complained. "I would have recognized that in an instant, in the old days. Come, child. We must hurry. It will snow again in a few hours."

They made an erratic way through the narrow strip of forest, which loomed above them on their left and fell away into a sheer drop on their right. Treetops stood on their level, and Choria kept a part of her attention trained there. Sometimes an unwary bird could be found venturing forth in winter.

Not all Willowill's pouncing was as fruitless as the first. They rooted out two snow hares and a large squirrel of a type strange to the Makra. They also uprooted a sleeping serpent, which the old woman added to her bag of assorted meat creatures.

Choria chuckled. "It would be good to let me dress out that one, Willowill, before taking it into the house. Theora would never touch serpent meat if she knew beforehand what it was."

The old woman snorted. "She will learn more things than eating meat not to her taste, while she stays with me. Let me be, child. I know what I am doing."

But when Theora was required to dress out the bounty of their hunting, Choria had many doubts of that. Theora hated getting her hands bloodied. The animals were bad enough, but when she thrust her hand into the bottom of the bag and touched the snake, she shrieked as if she might be under torture.

"It is meat. Attend to it," Willowill said shortly. "If you intend to eat beneath this roof, you will bear your part in the labor of finding or preparing it."

Theora looked with hatred at the old woman, then at her sister. Choria felt it in her heart to pity her sister for a moment. This was not, in truth, the duty for which she had been trained. But there was justice in Willowill's words. Theora needed to learn that food did not leap into her hands effortlessly. She had to realize that servants were a luxury, not a necessity.

It was the first of many bitter lessons for the girl. As the long winter dragged past into a delayed spring, Willowill demanded more and more of her guests. Choria hunted alone, as soon as the snow diminished. Theora found her hands grown sandpapery, her face blistered with heat from the cooking fire. The delicate beauty she had been so proud of took on an earthier quality that Choria found more attractive. Theora disagreed.

As soon as thaw was well advanced, sending the slides down the steeps and the streams out of their banks, Theora was ready to leave their temporary home. Anything, she insisted, had to be better than living with this ancient crone.

The strange contentment of the winter had also left Choria. She, too, was ready to go forward toward Algonath. Vigor raced along her limbs and through her mind. Some task awaited her, on the other side of this mountain range.

CHAPTER FOURTEEN

They said good-bye to Willowill beneath a watery spring sky. The soil beneath their feet was spongy, and the boulders along the precipitous path were gleaming with coppery and jade glints, all newly washed by the rigors of winter.

The air was chilly but invigorating, and Choria stepped out boldly. To her surprise, Theora did not lag timidly behind, as she had done before. It was no worry, now, to make certain she could keep up. Her winter of hard work had strengthened her lazy body, peeled away the layer of soft flesh that had enwrapped her. Her gaze was clearer, her step firmer than it had ever been before in her life.

Her disposition had not improved at all. "If you had not taken away our Gift," she muttered, "we could have transported ourselves to our goal at once, without having to tramp weary miles through these rough mountains!"

Choria had learned long since not to argue with her. She trudged forward, letting Theora natter.

But when time came to camp, she found her life much easier. The lesson in earning what you eat had taken root in Theora's mind, and she helped to prepare their supper without complaint.

It made the journey much easier, though they had many leagues to go before they reached the slopes of meadow that pastured the herds of Algonath. No herds grazed there now. There was no smoke from shepherds' huts tucked into crannies of the hills. Lower, in the fields where planting should have, begun, there were few furrows plowed. As they came through evening light, they could see four small houses strung along their path. Only one had lighted windows.

"I think your...enterprise...of last year took its toll," said Choria. "War has walked here, or I am badly mistaken."

They approached the lighted house and hailed long before they came near it. The light was quenched at once.

"We have little left," shouted a gruff voice. "And what we have, we will keep. Be gone with you from our door, looting filth!"

"We are two young women, traveling to find our kin," called Choria. "May we shelter in your shed? The night is chill, and the soil is damp."

There was a long pause. Then, "Come into the light, slowly. Best there be none tagging behind you to try surprising us!"

"We are quite alone," said Choria, moving into the long streak of light shining from the half-open doorway.

Theora followed reluctantly. They stood together in the light for several moments. Choria felt certain that someone had slipped from a rear door or window to check all about the house for any marauder who might be using the two girls as bait. She approved the strategy wholeheartedly.

After a time, the voice said, "You may come. One at a time. Still slowly."

She obeyed, and Theora came behind her at some distance. She moved through the door and stood blinking in the light inside the house.

It was a typical farmer's cot, formed in a square about an inner court, with a well and kitchen garden behind, she was sure. Stoutly built, it was furnished still with what fixtures had been built into it. Movable furniture was missing, and Choria knew that soldiers had, indeed, looted here. It made her fume to think they were probably from her own country, sent by her own sister.

"What has happened here?" came a voice behind her. Theora's. The poor creature could send men off to war without having the faintest notion what that meant to anyone.

Choria wanted to tell her—but she waited. Others would do that and would be believed far more readily than she.

"War has happened here, foolish woman!" came the reply. A big, rawboned woman came into view around a tall chest. She held a knobbed club in her hand, and she looked well able to use it. "Where soldiers go, ruin follows, always. Where have you lived your days that you've not learned such a basic truth as that?"

Choria hastened to reply. She wanted no hint of their identities loosed for bitter folk to chew upon.

"We have wintered in the mountains. We were caught there by the early blizzard and were unable to come home...."—Here she glared meaningfully at Theora—"...until the avalanches were over and the passes clear."

The woman grinned. "You do look a bit worn and weathered. Winter in the high places is nothing for the weakly to try. I take it that you found shelter, or you'd not be standing here."

"We did. And we gave fair return for the hospitality offered to us, believe that, dame. We are more than willing to do the same for you, in return for a night's rest in a warm place."

The woman frowned thoughtfully. Her squinted green eyes turned toward a rear door. "My son is ill. He has not been able to tend the beasts in days, and that task goes hard for me, for I ache with rheumatism. If, tomorrow, you will care for my livestock, I'll share with you our supper and our roof," She put the stick carefully behind the tall chest. "You may call me Vanori."

Choria could feel Theora glowering at her back. They had exchanged one kind of servitude for another, which must rankle the Makrala's feelings terribly. But Theora had not learned all the lessons such things can teach. Choria nodded briskly.

"We will be more than glad. And my sister will clean your house in the morning, while I go about seeing to the cattle. She is a master hand at such tasks." That was true, too. Willowill had taught her well, if impatiently, until she was as expert as any who had done household tasks all her life.

The sun was well down. Night had moved into the lowlands as the light was blocked by the mountains to the west. Choria brought wood to replenish Vanori's stock in her wood box, while Theora helped to peel vegetables and chop meat. They ate better than well, that night.

"You managed to save much of your store of food," she observed, as the three cleared away the remnants of the food and the dirtied trenchers.

Vanori laughed. "I have known wars before this one," she replied. "As soon as the first alarum is sounded from the peaks, up there, I drive the cattle into the foothills, bury all the vegetables that will keep, and put the perishables down the well. Anyone who allows herself to be caught with a house full of food by a marauding army is seven kinds of a fool."

"I had not known that Sherath had battered at our doors before this," said Choria.

"Well, why should you? For they have not come from that direction, our former enemies," Vanori replied. "South and west of us, as you well know, lies Starron. Due west is Kerrion. Both look greedily upon our lush fields, our splendid handicrafts, and our rich city. You have evidently not seen the city. Are your folk farmers, then?"

Choria was taken aback. Thinking quickly, she sighed.

"No. Our folk were weavers of a strange kind of silk. My father tended the small creatures that spun their webs into balls. My brother was unsurpassed at unrolling those into long, strong, fine strands. Our grandmother wove it with consummate skill into stuff used for many purposes. We lived well, but we did not have time to go into the city. That was the task of our grandfather."

She was astonished at the ease with which the string of lies rolled from her tongue. It troubled her. Was that another Makraitis fault, just now coming to light in her character?

Vanori looked up, her eyes alight. "I have heard of the family. A wonderful gift they have. But you speak as if they were gone, and I have not heard that."

"Oh, most are still alive and well, but our father sickened in the summer and died in the fall. We had gone to find kin in the mountains—he had left them a token, which we wanted to deliver. We had not expected such a sudden harsh winter. That trapped us there, and we have heard nothing from our family since."

The woman polished the last trencher and placed the shining wooden piece in its rack with the rest. "They should be well. The invaders came only from the west and the south. The area north of Algon is still untouched. Indeed, they did far less damage than the other armies that have crossed us through the years. They moved like slaves instead of conquerors."

"As if they did not want to fight this war?" That was Choria, who nudged Theora sharply as her mouth began to open.

"Yes. Just so. They returned westward joyfully, when they stopped their advance. It was as if someone had spoken a word, freeing them, and they turned and made for their homes."

Choria looked sidelong at Theora. Both knew what had happened. The moment Theora had lost her power, the collars had lost their ability to coerce those who wore them. Freed, they had turned in their tracks. How many, she wondered, had lived to see Sherath again?

"And were many killed, while the war lasted?" she asked.

"Fewer than I would have thought. We nursed many here, for a battle took place down the valley. Our men were cared for first, of course, but we also took in several of those others. They were properly grateful and soft-spoken. One I quite took to. A tall, wiry fellow with a head of hair the color of dried barleycorn. What was his name? Ahh. Bethor, they called him. Had he not been an enemy, I might have offered him my younger daughter as bait to keep him here on the farm. He seemed to like the life."

Choria's heart had given a great thump as Vanori spoke. She had thought surely that Bethor had perished in that last battle, though she had been unable to find his body. How had it happened that he was alive and in Theora's army?

She took the big pan of dirty water in both hands. "I will go and put this on the garden plot," she said. "Theora can come and see if the early squash are ripening. I see your vines growing tall. With rheumatism, it would be hard for you to stoop to pick them."

Vanori nodded absently, and the two went out the rear door toward the flourishing garden behind the house. Choria waited until they were well away from the door before speaking. "Did you know that Bethor still lived?"

Theora laughed, a bit nervously. "Of course. How could I not know that Garrier's son was taken captive? He had been knocked unconscious in that last battle, when your men were all killed. I thought it only just to send him off to do battle for me. You should have seen his expression when the collar was fastened about his neck."

Choria flung the water onto the first row of cabbages in the garden, restraining herself with some effort from putting it all over her sister. Then she turned to face Theora. "And you laugh about that?"

The girl was a bit pale. Her laughter was, Choria realized, that of nervousness. Theora was, indeed, frightened. Choria knew that her own expression must be strange and unusual. Nothing that she had done, thus far, had made her sister fear her.

Indeed, she made herself afraid. Her fury was enormous. Thinking of Bethor, bound by that foul collar, being forced to do Theora's unlawful work, made her ill. She wished, for a burning moment, that she had left Theora to be crushed in the fall of the House of the Makraitis. Better to let this flawed member of the family go down with the home that had nurtured her.

With an effort, she overcame the first and worst of her anger. Swallowing hard, she turned to go into the house again. The sky had darkened, now, and the last of the high clouds had lost their rosy glow. Night would find her trapped here with this heartless sister with whom she had burdened herself.

They slept on their bedrolls on either side of the hearth. The warm stone was comforting to Choria's bones, and she was grateful that she had no need to share body heat with Theora. The thought sickened her. Before she went to sleep, she thought again of Bethor. He lived. That was a thing that she had not had time to feel, to know, to understand. The big brother he had seemed in her childhood had become a staunch friend and comrade. Now it seemed that she wanted something more—if she could find him again. But he had gone, she felt sure, back toward Sherath.

She turned and rewrapped her covering. She could not go after him. She felt all through her that her work, whatever it might be, was here in Algonath. She had wondered, often, in the months since bringing down Theora from the High Seat, what that task might be. She turned again, then sat in the darkness and stared across the span of floor toward Theora. Could it be that her sole task was to do the thing her father had been unable to do? Was it her duty to turn Theora into a human being?

CHAPTER FIFTEEN

Morning found Choria anxious to travel. Vanori's farm would not have been a bad place to take up residence, but the Makra felt that her sister had already learned the lessons it might have taught her—and Theora's temper and tongue might well get them into deep trouble, if she let slip the fact that they had been the two Makra of Sherath.

So she asked Vanori as much as she could about Bethor, without being too direct about it, as well as drawing from her, very subtly, directions to the city and the area to its north where her bogus family might live. It was fairly easy. Vanori was open and unsuspicious, once she knew them to be harmless. When they left the farm, Choria had a fair notion of her direction.

They followed the long rolls of meadow and field that sloped easily downward. Strips of woodland divided the farms as they proceeded, and brooks and runnels crossed the track they followed. Choria knew that a river must lie at the low area at the foot of these descending slopes. The City of Algon lay beyond that river, protected on its western edge by the deep waters. She had learned that as part of her training as Makra, and as she progressed, she found herself recognizing areas she had read about in her studies.

As no other plan had presented itself, she intended to find that family—Spinnerrl, they called themselves now, though the name had been otherwise in times past—that had woven her gift from Bethor, and for years had been marriage-kin to him. She still wore that sash, bound about her waist beneath her tunic. It seemed the last trace of security or the past in this world that had turned upside down.

She had not confided her plan to Theora. The Makrala seemed to give no thought to ultimate destinations. She tagged persistently behind her sister, taking advantage of her strength and training, complaining bitterly from time to time, but asking no questions.

So they moved down through the farmlands to the truck gardens that supplied the immediate wants of the city. They found the river, looping lazily through a valley as green as that below Sherath. Orchards were beginning to show buds of pink and white as the two approached the ferry that served as the principal road into Algon from the west.

War had walked there before them, it was plain. The gardens were marked by pits and gashes, where opposing troops had dug in for long engagements. The orchard trees had branches lopped, trunks slashed. But spring was healing their wounds, and the gardens were all planted again, beginning to show a fur of green against the dark-turned rows.

The ferry, when they reached its docking place, was against the other shore. Choria sat on a stone mooring and watched, while Theora grumbled about the damage to her skirt and stood. The craft pulled itself back across the river, along heavy cables fixed to tall posts set into the banks. The pilot was very young—hardly more than a child.

She recalled the name she had learned. "You must be the son—or grandson perhaps?—of old Gunwold. How is it that you are working the ferry?"

The boy stared at her grimly. "I, too, am called Gunwold. My father and my grandsire are gone, dead in the war. Only I am left to ferry men and goods across the

89

river. I do not remember you—what family do you belong to?"

"I am going to see the Spinnerrl. We spent the winter in the mountains. I am sorry about your family—your grandsire had a fine reputation, and he will be missed."

The boy raised his hand, and the low rail across the front of the ferry was lowered for a pair of carts and a laden horse. The low raft sank even lower beneath the weight of its burden, and the draft beasts snorted as it swung into the current.

The city drew nearer, and Choria studied it with interest. Terraces of warehouses and shops rose from the river up a low ridge. There was an upthrust of stone at the top of that ridge, and it was crowned with white and scarlet roofs. There stood the homes of the wealthy. On its highest point was the Pavilion of Princes, home of the ruling house of Algonath.

From her position on the river, Choria could see a network of narrow streets as dark lines against the pale stone of which the city was built. They showed no damage nor marks of fire. The battle must have been fought beyond the river. She had removed the power from Theora's hands only just in time to save the city.

The river was broad at this point. It took half an hour to make the crossing, and all that while Choria studied the farther bank, while Theora stood by her side, wordless, staring, too. As they crunched onto the landing bar, and the rail went down, Choria spoke. "We will take that road along the riverbank. It leads northward. I have no wish to go into the city. There well might be someone there who could recognize you—or even me. That would be unfortunate for both of us."

As the girls stepped from the ferry, Choria reached into a pouch and took out the single coin she possessed that had been minted in Algonath.

"I hope that is enough—I have not ridden the ferry before, having lived beyond the river. My good wishes to you, young Gunwold."

Then she strode away northward, along the track skirting the river. Shops and warehouses straggled along at her right, and a few wharves thrust out into the water on her left. Fishermen dried nets in the afternoon sun, and Choria stopped to purchase a small net of fish with some copper she found in her pocket. Such small coins were not suspect, as they had always gone freely between the neighboring countries.

Before evening, she and her sister had walked clear of the outlying parts of the city, finding water meadows spreading across their way as the river looped away from the ridge. Lines of willows marked the courses of the many streams, and between those were low ridges and mounds of higher ground. The track lay along a continuous ridge, which Choria felt must have been made by human hands. It showed signs of being well traveled.

She kept watching for a likely spot to spend the night. She knew all too well the sort of companions that might crawl from the streams and the swampy spots to keep them company, so she passed many dry places that were too near the water.

They found a suitable place at last—not a moment too soon, as Theora was muttering and complaining more and more loudly. She was not over-pleased with the location of their camp, when at last it was found. She made that quite clear, as she helped Choria find dried willow branches for their fire. But she did help. The thought of raw fish did not tempt her palate, but she knew that Choria would eat it uncomplainingly rather than do all the work and let Theora sit idly and eat.

"Why do you want to see those people—the ones who spin silk?" she asked, when they had cleaned their hands and let the fire blaze up to light the darkness about them. "Artisans will be no help to us. We need rich men, now.

Only by marrying well can we assume places anything like those we have lost."

"You have lost. I never wanted such a place," replied Choria, placing fresh wood near the blaze. "And I have no wish to marry a rich man, either. I will, in the end, go as a mercenary, quite likely, once I get you settled. And until you learn to complain less and keep a pleasant expression, you will find no suitor, rich or poor. No man wants to be burdened with a whining wife."

Theora, for the first time, looked thoughtful. "I had not thought of that," she said. "What does a man want in a wife? I never expected to be faced with that problem. Only the problem of what I might want in a husband, if I ever decided to take one."

There was an unfamiliar note in her voice. Choria looked up into her sister's eyes. She had avoided doing that for almost all her life, for dangerous things had always lived there. Now she could see nothing that frightened her. Only inquiry and a bit of bewilderment.

She leaned her hand on her knee, staring across the blaze. "Do you truly want to know that? I cannot tell you much about it, for I have never considered marrying, for myself. But I have seen Garrier and his wife live together for many years. I have watched others, as I went about my quiet life in Sherath. I believe that I can tell you something. But it may not be to your liking."

Theora spread her bedroll and lay beside the fire, shivering as a night bird quavered in the branches of the willow beside their camp.

"Perhaps...perhaps it is time for you to tell me. It has come to me, at last, that I can never again be Makrala. I am not strong, as you have made yourself become. I cannot wield the power that was so dear to me. I cannot be a mercenary, as you can do, for I never trained for that. Nothing is left save to marry. You will not be troubled with me for long. I can see that plainly. You will give me a chance, and then, if I do not learn what is needful, you will leave me standing beside the road, one fine day."

Choria straightened. "If you are willing to listen, saying nothing, I will tell you what I have learned about people, women as well as men, and the ways in which they manage to live amicably together. But if you grow angry, begin your old habits. I will stop, and I will never speak of such things to you again."

The fire sputtered, as a damp branch caught. Theora bent her head to stare into the flames. Then she looked up again. "I will listen. Tell me what you know, however little it may be. I have known...that others did not like me. I tried to believe that it was because I was so far superior to them. But perhaps...perhaps the old woman in the mountains was not so far wrong. Am I flawed?"

Choria sighed. "You have been. Yet since we left Sherath, you have learned many things that I thought it impossible for you to learn. It may be that the flaw lay in the power you held within you. The power that I removed, along with my own, and laid beyond our reach.

"You are a different person, now. For the first time, I can look into your eyes without shivering. You are losing, it may be, the aura of that Makraitis Gift that went so terribly wrong with you, even in our mother's womb. You are now a person to whom I can talk. It may be that you are finding, at long last, the person you might have been had the Gift not been a part of your heritage."

The spring frogs trilled their peeping cries in the stream beyond the willows. Theora sat still, and a single tear slipped down her cheek.

"You never noticed the people," Choria went on. "They loved you, came to our door with flowers for you, adored you as the Heir, but I saw it. They did not catch *your* notice at all. So the things that became a part of me, as I grew up, never impinged upon you. Did you see the loving looks the women cast after their children? The caring gestures people made in the street? Old men would hurry after their old wives to share a burden. Young ones would reach shy hands to touch the sleeves of those they loved. Did you ever notice any of that?"

"No." The word was sad, soft.

Choria sighed. "I thought not. And those are the things that are most important if you are to live as a person, not as a Makrala. For a man wants what a woman wants—and how can I make you understand what I have only observed and never had time or opportunity to feel? Both want someone who cares at least as much for them as for themselves. They want a person who will be loyal to them, who will support them in time of grief or trouble.

"I think that wealth is not the most important thing, here. In fact, many of the most happy of our people had no wealth at all, simply knowing that there is one person in the world who is concerned, caring for them no matter what may happen. It takes someone who has thought of others to do that. Or someone who is determined to learn how to think of others. Do you think you can manage to do that? If you will try, I will stay with you as long as it is needful."

There was a long silence. Theora was watching the tiny flames dance over the red coals of their fire. She looked thoughtful. Sorrowful. Human, for the first time since Choria had known her.

At last she lifted her gaze to her sister's face. "Perhaps it is good that you took our Gift. I did not like being hated, though I hid that from myself and everyone else. I wanted someone to look at me as our father looked at you—as if you were very special to him. He never looked at me in that way, and I hated him for that. I thought I hated him for holding the power that would be mine. Now I think I know the truth."

She thrust a fresh willow stick into the fire. "You did not have to bring me with you. You did not have to carry me out of the House as it fell. You might easily have left me where I fell and gone about your life, unburdened by me. Why did you not do that?"

Choria poked the blaze, and tiny sparks flickered upward in the light breeze. Through that bright haze, she smiled at Theora.

"I suppose that I did it—because you are my sister. Because, in some strange way, I have always loved you, despite all our differences. Because I care what happens to you, however difficult you make it for me."

In the circle of firelight, the two sat silent. There was a different quality in that silence, now. It was a companionship of two linked lives, instead of being two separate silences.

CHAPTER SIXTEEN

Morning came with a gust of rain and a disgusted squawk from a family of birds in the willow. The sisters didn't try to revive the dead fire: that would have been hopeless. They chewed on bits of the hard journey bread Vanori had given them, as they trudged along the ever-muddier track leading northward. They met occasional travelers who were making their dampish ways toward the city. No one seemed to be going in their direction.

After a time, the ground along their bank of the stream began to rise. Their way was firmer, even though the rain did not abate. From time to time, a track led away from the river. On poles set into the ground were cryptic signs, naming the places to which the roads led. They passed a pole on which a wooden fish perched precariously. It seemed an unlikely spot for spinners of silk. They passed another, on which the rune that meant coal was burned. But at last they saw a hopeful sign.

This pole sported a fair representation of a hand loom. Choria turned off the river road onto the well-beaten track beside the post. This led into a complex of rounded hills crowned with low growths of odd-looking trees. After they had gone some miles along the twisting track, they found a small valley in which those strange trees grew in regular ranks. Already they were in leaf, and among them worked several children, who seemed to be gathering the leaves into bags.

Choria stopped and called to the nearest child, "We seek the Spinnerl. Can you direct us to their home?"

The small girl kept her hands busy cramming young leaves into her bag as she answered, "All t'village be Spinnerl. Go straight—any as you see will be Spinnerl, too."

It was simple enough. The sisters continued along the track, and soon they began to see paths wandering away among clumps of the trees to houses set well back from the public way. In many of the visible gardens sat women with lap-looms, their fingers busy.

Choria chose a modest but prosperous-looking house and turned to walk up its path. The two women busy in its garden looked up at the approach of the two young people. As she walked, Choria reached beneath her tunic and pulled loose the sash. Spreading it between her hands, she went to the older of the two women.

"Are you of the Spinnerrl?" she asked. "Those who wove this sash?"

"Let me see it," said the woman, putting out a hand curiously callused. She felt the web of cloth, drew it apart, snapped it into a narrow strip. Then she ran her fingers over the pattern of invisible knotting. A slight smile curved her lips.

"The one who wove that is now dead," she said, "but I know for whom it was made. I will not name him, for our land has been at war with his, but he is fondly remembered here." She stared closely at Choria, then at Theora. "And how did it come into your hands?"

"I was his student. It was his gift to me, when I attained all the skill that he could teach me. It is in my mind that there was more to the message woven there than I ever was able to decipher." Choria gestured toward a bench beside the table where the women had laid out shears and other equipment. "May we sit?"

"Indeed. There is good water in the pitcher, and the

cup is here." Neither woman had stopped weaving, except for the short space required for examining the webbing.

"I am seeking for that one for whom the sash was made. He was in Algonath before winter. We met one with whom he had stopped. Have you seen him since the war ended?"

The older woman's hands slowed. She studied the two young women closely again, as if judging them. The younger was not so cautious.

"What might have been the name of that one's father? We must, y'see, make certain you're no enemy of his," she asked.

Tears came into Choria's eyes, blink them back as she might. "Garrier," she said softly. "His father's name was Garrier, and his mother's was Lefsa. He, himself, was named for his mother's father. Believe me, Bethor is my friend. It may be that I have no other left in all the world but he—if he is still alive."

The older weaver's hands stilled on the loom. She drew her breath in a sharp gasp. "You must be—I dare not speak it. One from Sherath?"

"Two from Sherath. I am the Makra. My sister was the Makrala, and now she is simply a woman trying to learn to be a worthy one. Please believe that. Only recently have I begun to, but now I think it is true."

Now the other stopped weaving, as well, laying aside her roll of fine-spun thread and her small loom on which a sash to match Choria's own was taking shape. She stood abruptly, spilling a basket of bobbins. "It is dangerous...," she began.

"If this be Choria, then she is, indeed, Bethor's friend. We owe it to him to help her, no matter how dangerous it be. Show them into the house. I will put away the looms. Find a spot where they may hide, if the Searchers come. It is almost time, and the children in the trees may well betray these people to them," said the older. "Senneri! Control yourself. Do as I say."

Senneri gave a gasp, shook herself, and turned to go into the house. Choria followed, with Theora just behind her. She heard the door close behind them with a feeling of relaxation. It had felt entirely too exposed, there in the garden, when mention was made of Searchers. Choria could well imagine for what those Searchers might be looking.

"They are tracking down survivors of the invading army," she said, half to herself. "For what? Vengeance?"

The young woman sighed. "That, among other things. Our Lord was killed in that battle before the river. His brother-in-law and his Heir are at knives' points over his place. The searchers seek out not only those of the enemy who live, but also those among us of Algonath who are known to be for or against either of the claimants. That includes almost everyone, as you might suppose. It is dangerous to live here, now. It is dangerous to speak. It is dangerous to breathe...." She whispered the last words as the door opened and her mother came into the room.

"But the fearful never accomplish anything," that lady said quietly. "Put on the pot, Senneri. The children will come from the trees, soon, hungry for their meal. We will speak to them of discretion, then, though I fear it will be too late. Oh—check the secret way, before you do anything else. If any should...come looking...we will be alone." She spoke now to Choria.

"I am Cherras. Bethor was my friend and my husband's friend, as well as husband to my cousin. He aided us, long ago, when there was trouble from the east. My cousin made him that sash. She put into it the message Bethor requested, along with one of her own, to be read by our people, if ever the thing came back into our hands. She bade us befriend any who came bearing it." She sat beside a small table and began peeling vegetables for stew.

"If you are Choria, indeed, then Bethor has told us of

you."

"You have seen him!" Choria exclaimed. "When? Was it in the fall, when he left Vanori? Or since? I would dearly like to find him. Together, we might find a way home again. I have, I believe, begun the task for which I came into Algonath."

"He was here in early winter. We hid him for a time, until the Searchers became altogether too bold. When one has children, talk gets out, no matter how you caution them. We helped him escape by the secret way amid the first blizzard. He was going downriver, then across it and southward along the slopes of the mountains. There is a pass there that few attempt, even in summer. He was going to try it in the snow. We have worried about him since his dark shape disappeared in the swirls of snow."

Choria dropped into a low chair beside Cherras. Theora was already peeling vegetables, saying nothing, though her cheeks were more flushed than the small effort would explain. Choria knew that she was thinking of the cruel collar that had forced Bethor into a war that his soul hated.

"Then we will go south. How is it best to travel?"

Cherras poured her bowl of chopped squash and cabbage and potato into the pot Senneri held for her. When that was done, she turned to Choria. "This time of the year, too many travel the river road. And the lower you go along the river, the deeper and swifter it becomes. It is best to cross just north of the spot where our path diverges from the road. From there you can go through wide fields that have been broken to the plow but not yet planted, until you come to the toes of the mountains. Few make their homes there, preferring the lower elevations. You can travel along the lower ways, passing at night the great road that leads westward into Sherath. Six days hard walking after that passage, you should find the track leading up into the steeps. There lies the pass for which Bethor was making."

Choria nodded. "Is there game, there along the mountains' edges?"

"Little enough. The farmers begrudge the horned ones the little they crop from their fields. They hunt them fiercely and drive them up into the ranges. Food will be a problem, for you cannot spare the time to hunt. We will send what we can. And we will give your sister boy's clothing. She will never make that journey in skirts and petticoats."

When the children came in for their midday meal, Theora was neatly clad as a stripling. So slender was she that her shape did not belie her clothing. Choria, of course, was dressed in her leathers. The pack the women had made for them lay in a dark corner.

The small ones came in chattering, full of news. "While we picked the leaves for the worms, M'ma, two women came along the path. Junli spoke with them. And after a time, when they were gone for long, there came two men who asked many questions. They were very interested in those women. We think they're looking for them. They had stopped at Junli's house, when we came past. They will come here, when they are done asking at the other houses between." The little girl was pink with exertion and excitement.

"Then it is time. Take your packs. Senneri, lead them out by the secret way—to the river, mind you. Help them to find bundles of reed to form a raft for crossing, and take care. The Searchers do not distinguish between their own people and the enemy."

She took Choria's hands in her own. "Find Bethor," she said. "I have worried and fretted about him since he left us. I feel that he needs help. Find him, Choria. And may the gods give you aid."

CHAPTER SEVENTEEN

They slid out of a back window, dropping lightly onto a pile of mulch. It was raining again, more a mist than a downpour, and the leaves of the orchard behind the house dripped down their necks as they followed Senneri along the winding paths.

Behind them, where the road ran beyond the house, they heard a mutter of voices, clinkings, and clankings. The Searchers, they guessed, even as Senneri turned and laid her finger to her lips. They hurried after her through the wet trees and into a mass of greenery growing along a shallow stream.

Senneri stepped into the stream, after removing her shoes. Choria followed suit, as did Theora, and they moved as quietly as possible, sliding their feet along the pebbly bottom of the brook so as not to make splashes. From time to time a startled frog leaped from the bank with a yelp, or something slithered away into the ferns along the verge. Choria knew that Theora was shivering with fear, but there was nothing to be done. If her sister had learned to live in the real world, she would know what she was hearing. There would be no fear.

They were able to make good speed down the meandering stream, though Choria felt impatient at following its time-wasting loops and curves. But when she gestured toward the west, where the river should be only a relatively short distance away if approached in a straight line, Senneri shook her head violently. So they went on, damp and frustrated, listening always for the sound of pursuit.

At last, Senneri stepped out of the stream onto a wide lip of stone that thrust into the water from an outcrop forming one bank. Choria followed her and reached to help Theora. It was raining harder now, and the sun was down behind the clouds, so that darkness was closing in.

"They cannot hear us now," said their guide. "We are on the track leading to the river ford. Only the Spinnerl know of it—we have smuggled somewhat, in the past. Even the children know not to speak of it to any but those we can trust." She sat on the rock to put her shoes onto her pale and shriveled feet.

Choria hopped about donning her boots, and Theora pulled on her heavy leather shoes again. The path leading away from their position was studded with pebbles. To walk barefoot there would lame one quickly.

They moved along the path in near-darkness. Only Senneri's quiet steps guided them, as they stooped to miss overhanging branches and vines. This was evidently a trail made by wild things, not designed for the shapes of human beings. Their backs were stiff and sore by the time they emerged onto a dismal stretch of marshland. The north-south road ran, a pale glimmer, between their position and the river, which was a mere silver glint beyond it.

No one was in sight. They flitted across the soft stretch of land, across the harder surface of the road, and into the low bushes lining the riverbank.

Senneri was breathing hard, more with tension than weariness, Choria thought. "If only...," she muttered, casting about in the dimness and clutter. Then she caught her breath. "We are favored by the gods," she said softly. "The boat is here." And sure enough, a long shape showed dark against the damp vegetation in which it was concealed. They helped her to untangle it from the vines that had wrapped it about in their exuberant spring growth. The three stepped cautiously into the craft, and Senneri pushed off into the sluggish current.

Now they blessed the rain and the twilight. If anyone came along the road and stared toward the river, the low length of the boat would be hidden in the mist. They lay flat in its bottom, so as to make no silhouettes against the water. The Searchers might have left someone on watch at the ford, just below them.

When the craft bumped gently into the bushes on the other bank, nosing itself into their thickness, Choria smiled into the darkness. They had eluded the Searchers. They were across the river without having to swim, thus they would not begin a chill spring night both overtired and cold. Cherras's last blessing seemed to have some depth to it.

Choria caught the branch of a tree that leaned toward the water and pulled the boat to firm ground. Giving a hand to Theora, she helped her sister from the boat. Both turned to Senneri, who was almost invisible, now, in the early night.

"Our thanks to you, Senneri. And to your mother. May all the gods protect you and yours and bring peace again to your country."

The young woman reached up to catch their proffered hands. She gave them squeezes with her strangely calloused fingers, then caught up her oars again. "The gods go with you, Makra. Find Bethor. It is in my heart that he needs help. We have felt it, as my mother said. Find Bethor...," and she was gone, gliding quietly again onto the surface of the stream and into invisibility.

Theora had said nothing all the way from the house they had fled. Now she spoke and it was not of their flight. "Bethor—I had not known that he was so well liked. I thought that he was only Garrier's son. And Garrier was not of noble stock."

Choria turned on her. "Not of noble stock!" she hissed.

"What could be more noble than serving your ruler long and faithfully—than dying in the attempt to bring back the well-being of your country? And his son was trained in the same tradition. He taught me skills that few know among the younger warriors of Sherath. He cared for our family and our House with total dedication. Now he is adrift in a strange land that has warred with his own, and there is good reason to think that he is in peril. I trust Cherras—we knew her for only a few hours, but I'm sure that lady has a trace of the power."

Theora said nothing, only took up her pack and followed Choria as she made for the mountains, which were a slightly darker shade of black against the nighttime sky. As they moved cautiously across treacherous ground, Choria found time to wonder at the change in her sister.

She had fits of doubt as to the depth of that change from time to time. But Theora had learned something, there was no doubting. How deeply into her character that alteration had gone was a question that she was finding more and more reason to ponder.

CHAPTER EIGHTEEN

They came from the marshy lands onto plowed ground before midnight. There was no place to make a camp and sleep, so they trudged onward, their feet growing heavier and heavier with the mud picked up from the wet soil. Choria's bones felt sore, as if she had been beaten.

For all her rigorous training, her tough muscles and hardened skills, she was tired. She kept staring at the nearer skyline as they came into a place of low hills. Before long, she found what she had wanted—an outcrop of granite standing just below the crest of one of the hummocks that were growing more and more frequent.

"We will camp there," she said to Theora, just above a whisper. "We need a fire. To sleep damp, tonight, chilled and wet as we are, would invite illness. There, I think, we may be able to find deadwood and to hide the blaze."

The hummock was larger than it looked, and they stumbled over more than one smaller pile of rocks and boulders, making their way toward the one they had chosen. That one, when they reached it, was much larger than they had supposed.

A semicircle of boulders loomed about them as they crept into the shelter of the stones. Some immense shelf of rock had broken from the mountain, which was now very near. As it tumbled down the slopes toward the lower country, it had split into several segments, which had settled into almost a fan-shaped arrangement when they came

106

to rest. It was almost like a part of a fortress. Perfect for their needs.

"I will go and look for fuel. You can dig into the packs for food. We may face want later on, but we must be sure not to be ill now. We will eat well tonight," Choria said. Then she forged out into the pitchy night, leaving Theora in the tiny glimmer of flame they had coaxed from her tinderbox into a drift of dried leaves and grass caught in a cranny of their shelter.

She stumbled and cursed about the sloping hillock, finding small bushes, which she felt over for dead branches. A huge pile of such fuel would last only minutes, she knew. But finally she fell over a stump whose hacked top was of considerable girth. Someone had cut a tree here. There would be branches left, if she was lucky.

She returned to the stony fortress laden with roughly broken limbs. Theora was still nursing their flame along, using dried grasses she scavenged from every possible cranny. When they laid the first of the twigs on, then larger bits, she sighed with contentment.

"I never dreamed that a simple fire could be so wonderfully comforting," Theora said, as the two finished munching their meal of dried fruit, journey bread, and meat from Cherras's table. "Nothing that I ever had or did...before...pleased me as this does."

"Our father told you such things many times. You simply did not listen to him—or perhaps you thought that he was lying to you." Choria finished the last scrap of her meat and began edging the coals of the fire together, making a tight pile that would be easily kept burning through the night. She had made two more trips to the cut tree and had a big stack of wood drying on the other side of the flames.

Before Theora could reply, there came an interruption. "And what might be here? Two lads—no, by the gods! Females, alone and helpless in the night. Wanting the comfort of a stout lad, no doubt. Come, Helloren. We've our work cut out this night, I am convinced."

It was a rough voice, with a strange accent, neither Sheratha nor that of Algonath. Even as the words were spoken, two big fellows came scrambling down the northern side of the rock wall to stand staring at the sisters and their fire. Choria had not waited to see who or what they might be. She was on her feet, blade in hand. Theora, to her surprise, was behind her with her dagger drawn.

"Be careful with that thing!" Choria hissed over her shoulder. "I want none of it sticking through my gizzard!"

She turned her gaze upon the two facing her. "Two less helpless females you have never met, and if you desire to prove it, you have a rude surprise in store."

The taller of the two, a hulking man, indeed, made a lunge at her and drew back a cut hand as reward.

"That was not only stupid, it was inept. You cannot be soldiers. Now I wonder who and what you may be."

He sucked on his hand, staring at her owlishly. "We be Keren and Helloren. Brothers, indeed, out of northern Issaia. We signed on as mercenaries, you see, in Sherath and were sent here for war. We found it not to our liking and deserted. Then it looked to be the thing to sign on with the Searchers of Algonath." He sighed. "Not so. They be unpleasant folk, those Searchers, and we misliked the work we were made to do."

"What work?" The question was Theora's.

"Why, rounding up their own folk, as well as any straggle of enemies. Putting them to forced labor or, indeed, to the sword. Issaia be no tender place for coddling softlings, but it is better far than this. Think what ye will, we are no barbarians."

The big fellow's tone was so indignant that Choria almost laughed. A bit of rapine on the side was evidently not considered barbaric among the Issaians. She remembered little of her teaching on that score—Issaia was too distant and unimportant to be stressed.

"Then if you are not barbarians, you may share our fire and what we can spare of our food. You look to be lank."

Helloren, who had been silent, now spoke up, his tone the match for his brother's. "We do not take food from the mouths of lasses!" He went crawling back up the pile of rock and descended again with a pair of heavy packs. "We who're the sons of Rentor can provide for oursel's, look you. We did not leave the ranks of Searchers empty-handed. You may believe or no. Folk who steal from their own people deserve no better than to be stolen from, we hold."

Choria felt Theora nudging at her back. She knew what her sister was thinking—it seemed rash to offer camping place to these rough men. Yet Choria felt that it was safer to have them under their eyes and obligated to them, however slightly, than to have them mulling grudges in the dark. There was no sleep for anyone to be gained in that way.

"Then you are more than welcome," she said. "We are not hard-hearted with those who offer us no harm. Take your ease. Add wood to the fire, if you need to. We are weary past belief and must rest." She gestured to Theora, and they withdrew into the shadow of an overhang they had already chosen as their resting place. No rain could penetrate its depths—and no person could creep up behind them, as there was only one entryway into the cranny.

"Why did you let them stay?" hissed Theora, as they settled into their comers of the niche.

"Oh, I could have driven them away," Choria said, arranging her blanket roll. "But they would have suffered injured pride, the worst of things you can inflict upon a male. They'd have nursed their grudges, out there in the darkness. Before dawn we'd have had them trying to surprise us in our sleep. As it is, we can take turns, sleeping and watching. I think they will have to prove to us that they are not the barbarians they seemed at first. Another kind of pride, and a better one to my way of thinking."

She arranged herself comfortably, yet not so much so that she might fall asleep. "You roll up and sleep first, if you I will. I shall wake you when the time comes."

There seemed, truly, no need to watch. The brothers seemed well subdued, huddling close to the fire and eating their rank-smelling provender. They would glance, from time to time, toward the shelter of the women, but they made no move in that direction. At last, Keren banked the fire securely, and the two disappeared into another rock cranny on the farther side of the ring wall.

Choria allowed herself to drop into a light doze, though she didn't lie flat. She didn't wake Theora at all—indeed, she hadn't much faith in her sister's ability to stay awake or to assess any threat that appeared. Dawn walked up the east and threw first light on the mountaintop looming above the western side of the stone crescent, finding her awake but rested

"Theora! Time to wake up!"

Theora opened her eyes, saw the early light, and sat. "You didn't wake me!"

"There was no need. They're snoring away over there, gentle as lambs. We'll be gone when they rise."

They quietly arranged their packs, took journey bread for eating as they went, and crept from the semicircle. The snorers didn't rouse or even turn in their sleep.

Choria headed south, keeping to the steep slopes that were the knees of the mountains. The sun rose clear on her left as she led the way along the rough country that they now must traverse. Behind her, Theora kept the pace, uncomplaining.

"Six days hard walking, Cherras said," Choria remarked.

A ravine occupied them for an hour, scrambling down and crawling up the steep banks of the stream that poured from the mountains toward the river. Only when they were again on their way did Theora reply.

"I think we can make it," she said. "I...would like to find Bethor. I worry about him."

CHAPTER NINETEEN

The country was even rougher than Choria had expected. Ravines, tangles of downed trees left from winter storms, plowed land that they were forced to go around, so sticky was it with mud—these made a long journey of it. And, to be sure, they kept their attention partly turned behind. The sons of Rentor might have decided to be barbarians, after all.

Three days of hard walking found them still too far north, by Choria's reckoning. She made the difficult decision to travel at night, as well, though she knew that it would weary them, lessen their alertness, and possibly leave them open to unsuspected dangers.

Theora did not object when the subject was broached. She seemed subdued, totally unlike the sister that Choria had known all her life. She didn't quite trust this new Theora, though she devoutly wished to.

They fell into the habit of starting off in first light, walking hard until midday, then resting for a few hours before moving on. They would pause again at sundown, build a fire, and cook whatever they had been able to scrounge as they passed through the farmlands. Another few hours of rest would give them the energy to go on until the darkest hours past midnight. Only then would they sleep deeply.

There was no way in which they could set a guard. There was too little time for sleep as it was, and they simply had to risk whatever might come out of the darkness. They never slept in the place where they had built a fire. They both grew weary, scruffy, ill-tempered.

They passed the main western road just before midnight on the seventh day since striking their route. The strip of stone-paved track shone dimly gray in the starlight as the two darted across, their steps light and almost soundless. Tired as they were, they were only halfway to their goal, the little-known track leading up into the mountains.

Morning found them moving through land that was not under the plow. Wild country, overgrown with trees and brush, stretched upward along the slopes of the mountainsides. Spring was now well advanced, and they found ripening berries and wild fruit as they went. These made a welcome change from the dried stuff they had carefully apportioned to sustain them.

By midmorning, they had come into the cup of a small valley that ran from east to west across their way. They paused to rest and to eat a bit, and while they rested Choria kept looking to westward uneasily.

"What is it? Do you hear something?" Theora's tone was curious, not edging on hysteria, as it would have been only a few months before.

"There is a camp of some kind over there." She gestured toward a rough tumble of cliffs and forest. "I smell smoke. Do you not?"

Theora lifted her head and sniffed. Then she frowned. "I suppose I will never develop your skill. It is something that you must begin early, I think."

Choria nodded absently, her gaze still fixed on the area from which that faint tang was brought to them by the breeze. "I would like to look into that camp. It may be Searchers. It may be outlaws or deserters, like the sons of Rentor. I mislike passing by and leaving possible enemies to pick up our track."

Theora looked hard at her sister. "Do you think...? Is it possible that they might have Bethor?"

Choria turned to stare at her in surprise. "That is the sort of thinking I had thought you incapable of, sister. It is possible, but I think it unlikely. Surely, no one would have camped in such country through the bad weather. Bethor has been missing for some time."

"I am willing to go and see, if you are," Theora insisted.

"Good. We will take advantage of the rest of the day to work around to the south. It looks as if that area is so tangled and impassable they would never expect to be approached from that direction. There seems to be a cliff jutting out from that height—see where I point?—that would give us a perfect overview. Then we will know who and what they are. And, as well, if they hold any captives."

The sun was not yet past the zenith as the two slipped into the fir forest edging the valley. They went down and along a ravine for a considerable distance before Choria signaled to Theora to stop. She didn't speak, just gestured upward along a steep crevice that cut down to the trickle of water at the bottom of the gully.

They climbed up the steep way with some difficulty, but the top was reached at last, and they could look through a tangle of trees, some bent and broken by the weight of the snows of the winter past, toward the cliff Choria had seen from afar. Between it and the spot where they stood lay a chaos of broken stone, shattered trees, and gullied country.

It looked impassable, but Choria lay among the trees and surveyed the land for a long time, seeking for any indication that there might be a watcher on the height. After an hour, she decided there weren't any, and the two young women began the difficult traverse of the country between their ridge and the distant cliff.

It was dark when they finally stopped. They had covered perhaps half the necessary distance, and they were scratched, bruised, weary, and breathless. There was no water at hand, and they were more than glad of the small supply in their bottles as they smashed down enough of the tangle to make a camping place and dug out more of the dried fruit and meat for their lank stomachs.

They had found for themselves that it was impossible to go silently through the deadfall and brush, so they set no watch. Anyone approaching would announce himself long before he came near to the place where they slept. As the stars alternately shone forth and hid behind scudding cloud, they fell into exhausted sleep. The sky was showing a line of light in the east when Choria awoke.

Hard as the day before had been, their rest had gone deep. She felt ready for the new efforts this day would bring, and she touched Theora to wake her. To her surprise, her sister seemed fairly cheerful, though there was no water for washing and little food left to stay her growling stomach.

They started out as soon as there was light to see. The tangle seemed endless, but finally they stepped out of the saw-toothed vines and rough-broken tumble onto clean stone. It was the first step in a giant's staircase leading in angles and jogs up the height, which was the first real eminence at this part of the mountain chain.

Now their way was easier, though before their attack on the tangle they would have considered it very difficult, indeed. But there were no briers to catch their skin and clothing, mazes of broken trees and bushes to divert them from the direction they wanted to go. They could find almost always a ledge or a series of outcrops that would take them where they wanted to go.

By mid-afternoon, they were lying on the edge of the cliff, peering between boulders down into another cupped valley. This one had a small brook running down its lowest level. There were a few firs growing along it, where the soil was deep enough to hold their roots, and wildflowers bloomed rampantly, where they had not been trampled down by the feet of those who were making camp there.

Choria had no intention of stirring from her post until after dark, no matter what they saw in the dell below. Seven men were there, and from their glances off to the east, she thought they were expecting someone to come from that direction at any time. From her present location, the country lay like a map, and she could see the track they had taken. It followed the route of the stream, which had cut a gully in the stone of the mountain lying to the east.

The men seemed to have no immediate purpose except waiting. They wandered about the valley, dipped water from the brook, slashed idly at the wildflowers with sticks or blades, and watched and watched. Whoever was coming was important to them, there could be no doubt.

Although they lay some hundred or so feet above the camp, Choria could make out, quite soon, individuals among them. There was a short, stocky man who seemed to be the leader—it was he who shouted the orders, when anything was to be done. It was he who lashed one who was brought to him, hauled protesting between two of his fellows.

The afternoon was long. The sun sank behind the peaks, and shadows moved up the hills between that ridge and the valley. Just before full darkness fell, there was a bustle below. Someone was coming, at last, down that perilous path from the east.

CHAPTER TWENTY

Choria, as she waited, had surveyed her surroundings minutely. There was a faint track angling through a crack in a boulder, leading down to the valley. She was sure that it must be the path of a hare or other small animal, it was so small. But it would give a foothold, perhaps, to one going down the steep.

She was not at all certain that she could—or should—make the descent. But she was prepared for any possibility.

There came an increased bustle below. A campfire was kindled, and by its light she could see dark shapes moving into the camp. Four...five...six more. One of those carried something over its shoulder. Something suspiciously human-shaped. Something hanging too limply to be conscious—or alive? Six more, with the seven who had been there. Thirteen men—not good odds, if that limp shape should be Bethor's.

Now all the figures in the valley were grouped closely about the fire. Choria could see individuals, differentiating them by their clothing or their hair or their fanciful headgear, which ranged from turbans of rag to improvised hats woven, it looked, of vines and leaves.

The person they dumped roughly onto the ground beside the fire wore—a dress. A blue one, much torn and soiled. So, a woman had fallen into the hands of this bunch. Choria shuddered, and beside her she felt her sister

117

give a gasp.

The woman lay still. Was she, then, dead? But if she was, why had they troubled to bring her over that difficult path to the valley? Probably, she was unconscious.

The men stood about talking, for a time. One or two pushed at their captive with a foot, then desisted and wandered away to whatever sleeping place they had found for themselves. At last, only the leader and the tall, gaunt man who had led the incomers remained. They were talking quietly, it seemed, looking down, now and again, at the woman lying beside the fire.

Choria's mind was made up, without any conscious thought whatsoever. She would not leave that woman, whoever and whatever she might be, to the mercy of those below. From their looks, their behavior through the day, and the feel she had in her gut, she knew that the fate of any captive would be terrible, and that of a woman would be worse.

The two below moved away, at last, leaving their victim still limp beside the dying fire. As the wood broke apart, the coals died out, Choria whispered her plan to Theora. Then, though her sister's hand gripped hers hard, and her sister's quiet pleadings shook her, she slid over the edge of the cliff and set her toes into the narrow rabbit track.

It was breathless work, in the darkness, to feel her way down the almost perpendicular wall of rock. Only the wearing and breakings-away of the stone in the years of weather allowed her to complete her descent at all. As it was, she felt a bit dizzy by the time she was at the bottom.

There she found herself screened from the valley by a growth of bushes along the brook. Using them for cover, she slid into the water and moved upstream to the point near the remnants of the fire. It was now almost dead, only a spark or two still gleaming red but casting no light at all.

She crawled out of the water, feeling before her to

avoid any pots or buckets the campers might have left. The red sparks of the fire held their glow, keeping her oriented toward her goal.

The woman lay between the fire and the brook. As she neared the place, Choria grew even more cautious. Her groping hands found the cloth of the woman's dress, and for a moment she thought it was only another bit of debris from the careless habits of the men in camp. Then she felt skin, and the bundle beneath her hands gave a gasp of fear.

"Sssssss!" hissed Choria. She found the woman's hand and lowered her lips near the invisible ear. "Friend. Come me with me—while we can get away."

The head nodded vigorously, and the woman moved cautiously to her hands and knees. She caught hold of Choria's leather jerkin and followed her on the long, nerve-wracking journey back into the stream.

The water was cold, and the woman's teeth began to chatter. Choria felt that it was as much with nervousness as with chill, but she said nothing. Few women were prepared to undertake such a task as now lay before them. She was glad that it was too dark for her companion to see the cliff they had to climb before daybreak.

She had marked the spot where she came into the stream by breaking a branch and laying it perpendicular to the line of the water. She kept feeling along the bank for it, as they moved. At last, her hand found it. She held the other behind her to stop the woman. "Out. Here," she breathed.

Carefully, so as not to make any splash, they came out of the brook and through the screen of bushes. Choria felt with her hands to locate the stones she had memorized as markers of the spot for beginning the return climb. After an agonizing time of failure, she found the first, then the second. Between them, there lay the first set of hand and footholds.

Now it was time to talk with the woman she had rescued. She put her lips near her waiting ear and said, "We must climb now. It is difficult, but not impossible. Follow me. Feel where my foot goes, each time. Set your hands in my footholds, your feet where your hands have been. You must remember. You must concentrate. You must not think what you are doing. Just follow. It is the only way— unless you want to go back there."

"I will," It was only a breath, but it seemed to hold determination.

Choria turned and attacked the cliff. As she moved upward, slowly, cautiously, she heard the scrabble of the woman's hands and feet behind her. More than once there was a gasp of fear as a hold was missed or crumbled a bit beneath her weight, but they both moved up the cliff, yard by yard.

"Theora!" It was little more than a whisper, but Theora heard it.

"Here. My hand is out, if you can find it. It is too dark to see."

Choria felt upward, waving her own hand along the stone as high as she could reach. When she had moved upward another pair of steps, she felt the breeze of Theora's hand passing. She reached again, caught, and was helped over edge of the split boulder. They both reached down to help the woman onto the ledge. She was exhausted and breathless.

"We must move, and now," Choria said softly. "They will look where they have not looked before, when you are missed. What may we call you?"

The woman had sunk onto a boulder, panting from effort. Soon she controlled her breathing enough to reply.

"Call me...Pedrada. It does as well as any."

Chona had an odd feeling. "Pedrada? The Lost One. Lost from where, lady?"

"Do not ask. Not now, at least. If we must move, we must move now, for I do not know how long I can make my limbs follow my will."

"So be it. Theora, you take the lead. We will go south, now. See that planet hanging over the peak there? Guide yourself by it. It will move slowly to your right, but keep correcting your course by the peaks, as well. We will not go the way we came. It is too slow, and we left a trail—that could not be helped. We can go more speedily along the rocky ways, and they will not expect that route." Choria was thinking both ahead and behind, as she had been used to doing through the years of campaigning.

They moved out, Theora ahead, Pedrada behind her, Choria bringing up the rear, as the best warrior, if any should pursue them closely.

They moved slowly, because of the darkness, but the starlight was helpful before long, as the clouds blew away over the horizon, leaving the sky clear. Then the pale boulders were easily seen and avoided, and the ink-dark paths more easily detected.

By daybreak, they were going along a high trail that skirted the edge of another mountain. It was so stony that there was no chance of their leaving traces of their passing. They didn't pause, but kept moving until they found a track leading lower.

"We must go down, now," Choria said. Even she was weary to the centers of her bones, and she could see that Theora was going upon nerve alone. The woman, Pedrada, was walking automatically, stiffly. Choria found herself admiring the older woman's determination.

They followed Theora, wearily, down the narrow path that was paved with rubble fallen from the mountainside. It led into a wooded dell. Another stream bubbled there, carrying away the snow water of the previous winter. It was sheltered, hidden from any who moved either on the path or lower.

"Here we will rest," Choria said, dropping her pack and sitting on it.

Theora fell flat onto the damp ground. Her breathing was labored, and Choria could see her legs jerking with the stress of heir long trek.

Pedrada stood, dead on her feet, until Choria reached up and pulled her down. She sank onto her haunches, rolled onto her side, and was asleep before she was fully extended.

* * * * * * *

It was almost noon. The sunlight was blocked by the thick-needled firs, as well as the birches growing along the stream wherever there was a chance of sun. Choria knew that they must rest now, in order to be prepared for whatever would come later.

She could not believe that those in the valley would not search hard and long for the woman they had captured. The more she thought, the more she believed that Pedrada was one who mattered here in Algonath. The entire atmosphere of the camp she had watched had changed when she had been brought there.

She studied the sleeping woman's face. She should have been resting, she knew, but her mind was turning over all that she knew and had observed in the past two days. This was not the face of a simple dame, content to work at farming or spinning or housework. The hands, though scratched now, and the nails broken by her climb the night before, had been finely kept beneath the grime. The face held intelligence, humor, and a hint of command.

Pedrada—the name reminded her of one she had heard before. That of the Lady Mother of Algonath—Petriana. She stared at the sleeping countenance. The line of the skull was beautiful beneath the aging skin. The hair still retained a chestnut luster, though it was beginning to streak with gray. Nothing there was unlike the descriptions she had heard of Petriana.

Satisfied, Choria turned on her side and drifted into sleep.

CHAPTER TWENTY-ONE

The chirrup of a night bird woke Choria at last. She opened her eyes and glanced about her without moving. Was it a real bird, or did some pursuer signal so to his fellows?

There was nothing suspicious within range of her vision, so she sat and stretched quietly. Her two companions were still sleeping, as she could tell by their even breathing. She could see only dark bulks and darker ones in the dell, but none of those moved more than the light breeze would justify. The bird, she could now tell, was in a tree almost above her. She sighed and stood, moving cautiously between Theora and Pedrada to gain the bank of ferns that hid the dell from the path. Sinking to her hands and knees, she crawled through the cool growth, her ears pricked to their utmost. When the pebbles of the path could be felt beneath her palms, she stopped and stood again. Listened. Only sounds natural to the night reached her.

She felt her way back to her sleeping place. She felt an urgent need to move on, but she knew that such blind fleeing through the dark, and in unfamiliar country, was not an intelligent thing to do. They were hidden. Their tracks, along the ways they had come for miles upon miles, were undetectable to the keenest tracker—she had checked along their back trail from time to time as they went.

No. They must rest. When it grew light, they must decide upon a course and pursue it with care and determination. She had a feeling that Pedrada had her own needs and duties, and those, too, must be investigated and satisfied, if possible.

With the discipline learned through most of her life, she lay again, her head upon her pack, and slept. She did not wake until there was light starring the tree canopy above her.

Pedrada was sitting, staring over at her with interest. "So. My rescuer is no tough and seasoned warrior, but only a child!" she said, her tone amused.

"No child," objected Choria. "I have been a warrior since I was thirteen. I am—was—the Makra Choria, out of Sherath. This is my sister, the former Makrala Theora. We are making a journey of...restitution."

Pedrada's eyes narrowed. "And how did that come about? Your forces conquered ours, without any doubt. What caused conquerors to decide upon such a strange action?"

Theora had waked, but had been lying quiet, listening. Now she spoke. "My sister fought me, every step. When she returned from her short exile, she came to me and took from me all the power inherent in the Makraitis, and, as well, she divested herself of her own. A foolish thing, I thought it at the time, but now I am beginning to see that the power divides us from others. We do not understand them—or I did not—as we should." Her voice became husky, and she cleared her throat impatiently.

"Choria brought down the House of the Makraitis. When she took my power, she freed all those I had sent under compulsion into Algonath. Though the battle was won, as we have found, the army divided into individuals who had never wanted to come here and now only desired to go home again."

Theora rubbed her grimy hands over her face and frowned. "I must wash!" she said. "How fortunate there is a stream here."

"And why did she come here and bring you?" asked Pedrada. "What restitution did you hope to make?"

Theora didn't answer but turned to the stream. Choria faced the woman and replied, "I didn't know, when I turned my steps here, what it was that I must accomplish. I was, quite simply, compelled to come. But now I know. I must find Bethor, my old friend and teacher in the warlike arts, and make certain that all is well with him. Every person we have met who knows him is worried. As I am."

Lines of amusement wrinkled around Pedrada's eyes. "Friend, teacher—and something else, I think," she mused. "The name of Bethor is one I know. I was held for a short while in a camp south of—here? I cannot say. I was unconscious for most of the journey to that place where you found me. It was far south of the western road, that I know. He was held, with some score of others, by the Searchers."

Choria straightened abruptly. "But—if you are the person I think you, the Searchers should never have troubled you. Indeed, they should have obeyed you, instead of taking you captive."

Pedrada sighed. "So. You have guessed. Yes. I am Petriana. Mother of the Lord of Algonath. Grandmother of the Heir. Not, thank all the gods, mother to that uncle of the Heir who is trying to seize control of our unhappy country. He is the brother of my son's wife. Kelldron is his name, and he is filled with ambition, lacking any trace of compassion. He finds me a pawn worth using. So, I am grieved to say, does my grandson, though he is too young to understand fully what it is that he is doing."

"Ah. You are in some way being used to lever power from the Council?" asked Choria.

"I was adviser to my son, as to my husband. The Council values my words and will not approve as the true ruler of Algonath anyone, heir or other, of whom I do not approve, myself. Kelldron knows that I would never approve him."

She lowered her head and stared at the loamy soil. "He ordered the Searchers to find and seize me. He hopes to force me to give my consent to his elevation. But if I will not do that for my own grandson, I will most certainly not do it for an opportunist who takes advantage of his country's suffering to seize power. I am at odds with both of them. If I escape from one, I stand a fine chance of falling into the hands of the other. Either captivity is unlikely to lead to my survival. If I can be found dead—in some manner that cannot be proven to be unnatural—the Council must make a decision. Both hope to sway the Council, either with force or persuasion. As you can see, my position is a hopeless one."

Choria nodded, her mind busy. As she followed the woman to the stream to wash, she was thinking hard. By the time they had eaten the last remnants of food left from Cherras's store and their gleanings along the way, she had come to a conclusion.

"You must come back to Sherath with us," she said, wiping her hands and redoing her pack. "There is nothing for you here, just now. When all is settled, we can send word to the Council. By that time it will be clear who has won the rulership and how he is ruling. What do you think of my plan?"

Petriana laughed. "Wonderful! If we can escape from all the bands of Searchers who are ordered to find me. And if you can find your friend Bethor among all their camps. I would recognize it, if I saw it, but I could never lead you to it."

"We knew his direction. Unless they have moved him, he should still be where you saw him, and if that was south of that other camp, then it was along his planned route. We'll find him." Choria sounded a bit more confident than she felt. The mountains rose in rocky mazes and forested slopes. To find a single camp in such rough and unknown country was something that would require more luck than skill, she felt certain.

Theora had said nothing. Choria couldn't quite interpret the expression she wore—it seemed more pleased than the reverse, but with Theora you could never be quite sure. But, at least, she did not object to the plan.

"I don't know this land at all. Do you?" Choria asked the older woman.

"I used to hunt here, when I was a girl. I was trained here when I took my warrior training. Yes. I know these mountains—or I did, long years ago. Much has changed."

"Long ago is better than not at all," Choria said. "Bethor was going to take a pass that is seldom used. The trail leading to it cuts through the mountains six days' journey south of the western road. We were a bit more than a day south of the road when we turned west to investigate that camp. Now we have come at least two days' journey southward. Though we have, I will admit, wandered back and forth quite a lot. If we reached a high place, could you tell where we are? That might give us a notion how far it is to that other pass. I feel that the Searchers must have camped near it, to catch anyone trying to cut through that way."

Petriana nodded, her eyes thoughtful. "Let me but reach a goodly height, so that I can see the shapes of the peak around us, and I can tell you very nearly where we are with regard to that way. But to go back up—that may well put us into the way of those who will be searching for me."

Choria smiled, feeling her teeth against her lips, sharp and unamused. "They will think they are pursuing a lone and unskilled woman. You have had the training, even as I have. You are strong, or you would never have survived our trek or the climb before that, or probably the captivity before that. With the two of us, on those breakneck paths, no force could hope to come at us in strength. If they should find us, keep your pity for them."

Petriana's dark eyes filled with brightness. "I had not allowed myself to hope, after being dragged from my house, seeing my old servants slaughtered in my defense. I had only thought to escape into the wilderness and to die there, where no proof of my death could be brought back to the Council. Now I feel young again. My old skills are not lost. As you say, I am strong. We will go up, and I will show you the way we must go."

CHAPTER TWENTY-TWO

It was still early. Dew frosted the ferns as they pushed through them. Sunlight struck at an angle down through the birches and the firs. Birds were filled with late-spring glee and brightened the wood with their song, as the women found the path again and went up its steep and pebbly course to the ledge from which it had brought them.

"It isn't a path at all," observed Theora. "It is a watercourse. You can still see pools between the big rocks, if you look. Such runnels carry off the first and worst of the spring thaw. It should lead us up, by the easiest route, to some eminence tall enough to give us a view of the lands to the south and east. Westward, there will only be peak after peak, getting higher the farther west they go." Petriana strode upward, after the two girls followed her, glad of her certainty.

They crossed the ledge. Choria inspected it closely, but such rough terrain held no tracks. They went up the pebbly course of the runnel, stepping cautiously. A broken leg, at this point, might well doom them all. It was difficult going, and the higher they went, the more difficult it became.

Though the sun was burning brightly, the air grew cooler, for they were gaining altitude quickly. The wood below became a fuzz of mossy green. The ledge disappeared. The other mountains now loomed on their own level, instead of above them.

The runnel ran more steeply. Only the tough growth of bushes aided them in climbing it. Handholds were valuable, for the stones tended to roll underfoot. At the point where the watercourse disappeared beneath a pair of boulders, they stopped and turned to look back.

They seemed to stand on the roof of the world. The course of the river, tens of miles to the east, glittered in the morning sun, its loops marking their curves on the green fields and red-brown plowland. The City of Algon shone beyond it, toy roofs and walls almost invisible in the distance.

Nearer, tan-green slopes rolled up to meet the foothills. They could detect movement there, but whatever moved was too distant to identify.

Petriana turned south. A boulder blocked her view, so she climbed onto it and stood against the sky, hand shading her eyes, as she looked long and hard. When she came down, she looked pleased.

"I know how to go. We have saved some time by traveling so high. Going across the toes of the mountains cuts off miles of travel. And there is a road that I used to know—the ancient smuggler's road between our two nations. It leads to that same pass that Bethor attempted, but it approaches in an unexpected way. It had been forgotten when I hunted there and discovered it as a girl. With the forest's growth of years, it should be hidden well."

They moved down even more cautiously than they had climbed, for it is far more dangerous to descend. The convenient scrub helped them, and they came to a point some yards above the ledge they had used before, just as the sun was gone.

There were voices below. They sank silently to the stone. Listen as they might, they could distinguish no words from the mumbles and mutters along the ledge.

Choria put her mouth near Petriana's ear. "I must go down nearer, to see how many they are—and who they may be. While they may be Searchers, they may also be some who flee from them. I would not like to kill any who are innocent."

"Go, then. But take care. We are not so numerous that we can afford the loss of even one."

As she crept past Theora, her sister caught her arm in a tight grip. "Come back. Safely!" she breathed.

That was Choria's intention. She moved like a lizard, flowing over the pebbles so that they didn't shift. The cool mountain breeze chilled the sweat on her back and arms as she went. When she found an outcrop of rock a man-height above the ledge, she flattened herself there to listen.

"...waste of our good time!" she heard a shrill voice complain. "No old woman could come so far—and her out of her senses, too. I saw 'un, lying there by the fire. I saw that lump Dongerre laid alongside her skull, too. No, some beast o' the night come crawling and took her away. E'en now, she is a pile o' bloody bones in the brush, where none o' our kind will ever see her more."

"Well, we both know that, but Dongerre and Alsgard will have us look, sensible or no. Now come and be quiet. 'Twill be too dark to move soon, and this be a goodly spot for resting, so as not to fall from the mountain to our deaths." This was a deeper voice, touched with the farmer accent.

"And where is our good leader, then?" shrilled the other. "Past time, it is, for him to be here."

"He will be back in a bit. He followed the runnel down a way, just to see that none had used it as a path. He's no fool, is Karden. Sit and rest your bones, will ye?"

There was quiet for a time. Choria took the opportunity to flow back upward through the increasing darkness.

"Three," she whispered. "Two idiots, one who may have some sense. But they don't really think they're following anyone, just looking along every possible path."

"Then they'll expect no attack." To Choria's surprise,

that was Theora's voice.

"True." That was Petriana. "And we need no Searchers rambling about these heights, while we need to make haste to the south."

"The third should return soon. He looked below, and we left no trace of our stay in the dell. He will return, now that it is too dark to search well." Choria slid backward, found her former route, and moved back down the mountainside. Behind her she heard faint brushings of clothing against rock, sometimes a tiny click as two stones met beneath unaccustomed weight or pressure. Both of her companions moved like warriors toward their unsuspecting prey.

There was barely room for the three of them on her outcrop. Below them, three voices were now conversing carelessly about the quality of the beer in their jugs, the incompetence of leaders who sent men on such useless chases, and remarks on the looks and ancestry of each that none seemed to take amiss.

After a long time, there was quiet below. The tiny smudge of fire they had kindled from deadfall their leader brought from below died out, its glow ceasing to light the edge of the outcrop.

Still, they waited. When the constellation of the Shield stood above the nearest peak, Choria moved.

"I shall go down here. It is only a short drop, and I shall land amid them. You two take them from the runnel side." She slipped over the edge of the stone, hung by her hands for a long moment, then dropped softly onto the ledge below—onto an outstretched foot!

She waited for no more. Shrieking like a homeless spirit, she laid about her with her blade, striking blindly in the dimness. Then she heard other shrieks and moved back, so as to miss being injured by one of her companions.

Theora had her dagger. As a last spurt of flame flickered from the trodden fire, she saw that Petriana had armed herself with a rock and a stick. She was making do quite well with both.

A man lunged upright, and she kicked his feet from beneath him. He went over the edge, bouncing and yelling all the way down. The other two were still now. Petriana laid her stick amid the coals, and when it blazed up, they saw that Choria had taken one through the chest. Theora and the older woman had finished the third—he showed marks of both dagger and rock.

"They will be missed," said Choria.

"Yes, but their absence will be put down to desertion. Many have deserted, and many more will. The Searchers find themselves despised and shunned. Men do not like that."

Recalling the sons of Rentor, Choria realized that it was true. "Look in their packs," she said, setting her boot against first one and then the other of their victims, to push them over the edge after their comrade.

There was food in the packs that had been pushed back well against the steep side of the ledge. Meat and bread, even confections made of fruit cooked long with honey and spices. The three women made their first good meal in days. Then, there, where they had worked such havoc, they lay down and slept.

CHAPTER TWENTY-THREE

Petriana moved surely through the countryside, avoiding well-used paths and roads. The three covered more distance in their first day of travel together than Choria would have thought possible. Knowing where you were going helped a great deal.

They rounded the flank of the mountain along whose sides they had been traveling for so long. A long valley lay between its roots and the beginning of the next height, which reared itself to the south and east. The little river that flowed there offered baths and refills of the water bottles, but they didn't pause for long. The thought of Bethor pushed them forward.

There was more reason for this than simple intuition. The first night together, about their campfire, had been illuminating, for Petriana had told her story. "I will not tell of the day I was seized. I am still full of anger and grief concerning that," she said.

"But they overpowered me and carried me away with my head bundled into a bag. When they uncovered me, we were already across the fields and well into the foothills. From what they said, I knew they thought me to be a woman of the houses, knowing nothing of the lands about, and I did nothing to give them any other notion." She gazed into the fire, her expression sad.

"I was determined, if it were at all possible, to avenge my people, whom they killed. But it looked very hopeless.

I was alone, bound tightly, and tied onto the back of a pack beast. Nobody knew where I was, and I knew that my own grandson had intended seizing me, just as his uncle had done. Kelldron, being older and more experienced, had simply outmaneuvered him. I wanted none of either of them."

"They took you first to the camp where Bethor was?" asked Choria, trying to control the unevenness of her own voice.

"No. That was the third camp. They kept moving me about—probably as my grandson hunted for me and my kidnappers. The third camp was that one near the track to the pass. Bethor was there, and I had met him before. He was well known in the City, in the time of my Lord. It was like finding a friend in the wilderness. The fact of the war between our nations was forgotten. We were united in our contempt for those who held us captive. I managed to hide my feelings; Bethor didn't try to conceal his."

"He wouldn't," Choria chuckled. "It almost destroyed him, hiding his thoughts and his activities from Theora's people, while we waited for what must happen. We could never talk about it, however safe it seemed, for one never knew what nook might hold a pair of enemy ears."

Theora looked uncomfortable, and Petriana hid a smile of amusement. Choria, however, had long since stopped trying to save her sister's feelings. She waited for Petriana to go on with her tale.

"We were kept, with two others, in a sort of pen the Searchers had built of logs and stones. Those inside it were loosely shackled, but four men stayed on watch from a crag just above the enclosure. We could talk without being overheard, which was a comfort. Only Dongerre, of all those in the group of Searchers, seemed to have intelligence, and he was a careless sort. What he might have learned from us might have been worth something to him, but he seemed not to care for that.

"We said nothing for some hours, Bethor and I. Both of us were cautious until we realized that there was no need for that. Then we sat in the shade of a boulder and put our heads together. He had a tale of his own—of being enslaved to a collar controlled by...his Makrala. Being sent into a war he abhorred, among men as helpless as he to resist. He was bitter, make no mistake. And he was deeply concerned about the fate of the Makra Choria, for he had no way to know if she still lived.

"We spent much time, over the next week, trying to find a plan that would set us free. The other two captives were suspicious of us and of each other—they avoided everyone and would not talk with either of us. We watched our captors carefully, examined our surroundings over and over, and decided, at last, on a plan." She sighed.

"Before we could put it into effect, Dongerre brought in more men and put Bethor to the question. I never knew what they thought he knew or could tell them. When they were done, he was a wreck of a man. They brought him back into the compound, bleeding, unconscious, his flesh almost as tattered as his clothing. I was sponging the blood away, trying to find his worst wounds, when they came after me to take me away. I have never known what happened." She looked over the blaze into Choria's eyes. "He may be dead."

"No. I would know that, I think. I hadn't realized it before, I but now I feel inside myself that he still lives. We will find him." Choria's tone was confident. Irrationally, she felt that she was right.

Petriana stared intently. Then she gave a small nod. "Perhaps you are correct. I have no real knowledge of the severity of his wounds, and blood always seems so much more dangerous than the injuries it covers. We will find him."

The knowledge that Bethor might well be suffering still from the result of his beating spurred them on. They traveled from first light until long after it was really too dark to go safely, stopping seldom in the daylight hours to eat or to rest. They cut travel time from six days down to four.

They came upon Petriana's hidden way at midmorning. Only she would have recognized it as a road, for it was overgrown with bushes and vines and overhung by immense trees, watered by the stream running amid the lush growth along the bottom of a ravine. The heights hanging over it were distinctive, however, and neither of the sisters doubted that her story of them must be correct.

They rested in the cool shade until the sun sank behind the mountains on the west. As she sat soaking her feet the brook, Choria thought at last about the swift journey she and Theora had made from the house of the Spinnerl to this spot. So quickly had events piled, one upon the other, that it seemed unreal, even to her who had covered all those miles.

The sun was hidden all too quickly—the heights seemed to lean over the small canyon, and it was covered with shadow long before mid-afternoon. Petriana dried her feet and pulled on her shoes, sighing over the condition of her bruised toes and heels.

"They took me in the shoes I stood in, and they were not designed for traveling over rough ground. But I will go on—perhaps to make a pair of hide slippers from the skin of one of Dongerre's henchmen."

Theora stared at her, shocked. "Surely, that is not a sentiment for a gentlewoman to entertain!"

"The only gentlewoman worth knowing is one who can stand eye to eye with danger or demon and spit in its face," the older woman replied. "To be soft and gentle is fine, when there is a need for it. It is stupid when there is need for fortitude and determination. One must deal bloodily with the bloody-minded—that is all they know or understand. You will learn, young Makra, if you live so long."

Theora said nothing, just finished attaching her pack to her shoulders. Choria chuckled silently. Step by step, her sister was learning the things she should have accepted from those who taught her.

Choria had willingly handed over leadership of the trek to the elder lady. Petriana was one she could follow with confidence—she thought what a pity it was that she had been required to marry and rear children, when she would have been so fine a general. Little joy had her children brought to her!

They moved up the game track that followed the water. There was no sign that men had ever stepped there.

"Surely the smugglers did not use carts," Choria said softly, as they worked their way around an immense boulder that had fallen long ago to half block the stream and the path.

"No. They carried their goods on their backs, long files of them moving silently and invisibly through here, as I was told by one who had been a smuggler before joining my father's household. If he had not told me and brought me here, I would never have suspected the existence of this track. Probably no one else now living does. Here— we make a fishhook turn. Follow close after me when I disappear from view."

They scrambled around another boulder, and, sure enough, Petriana disappeared. Theora went after her, leaving Choria to come last. She found herself in a sort of half-tunnel dug into the bank of the stream by torrents of runoff from the snows of winter.

"This is the tricky part," their leader whispered. "Make no sound—we are going through the mountain, into the valley where that camp is—or was. This place carries any noise and amplifies it. So no more talking, and step carefully."

Choria could hear the faint whispers of sleeves or

shoes against rock go rushing away up the tunnel that branched her right. A breeze met her cheek as she turned into it, and she knew that it did, indeed, lead through the mountain. Had those long-ago smugglers dug it themselves? Or had nature formed the meandering, rough-walled way?

Things squeaked or slithered as they moved into the darkness. She was reminded, there in the gloom, of her trip beneath the ruined houses, back in Sherath. In a way, this was a better sort of trek—this time she had no fear riding within her that she would be forced to kill her sister.

They used no torch, though one could have been contrived and kindled easily. Someone might be on watch on the valley end, and they wanted no hint of their coming sent before them. Choria felt along the wall to her left, keeping her right hand on the hilt of her blade and following the faint sounds made by those in front. It seemed a very long way. They stopped once to rest and to eat. Her inner time sense told her that it was probably near to sunset, or perhaps a bit later, but there was no way to know with certainty.

Then it was literally hours of stepping cautiously along in total darkness, reassured only occasionally by a scuff of sound in front of her, or a drip of moisture falling into some hidden cup of rock. When her searching hand came up against Theora's back, and her sister's fingers reached back to squeeze hers in warning, she felt that she had been traveling for years instead of hours.

Petriana came back to join them. Without speaking, she touched their arms, guiding them around to the right, down a narrow ledge, where Choria's toes felt as if they were thrust out over a sheer drop. When she let them stop, at last, there was the feel of fresh air, the smell of firs and water. The stars were hanging low over a bulky peak nearby.

Between them, Petriana breathed, "There was no

guard. It may be that they know nothing of the tunnel, though a better leader than Dongerre would have checked every inch of this valley before setting up his camp here."

"Where is the camp?" asked Choria softly.

"Beyond the grove of trees that climbs partway up this wall of the valley. The enclosure is hidden by its wall—there is always a fire there, or torches are lit—or both. But the camp lies between us and the place where we may find Bethor. We must go through it. There is no way to go around. Believe that. Bethor and I memorized all of the places within range of our vision from the prison enclosure. The walls are sheer except for the path leading into this valley. That goes out to the main road, if you can call it that, over the pass."

"And how do we get down?" breathed Theora.

"Follow me," the woman answered.

Theora laid a hand on Petriana's shoulder. Choria laid a hand on her sister's. Together, moving their feet cautiously, they went along the ledge on which they stood until Petriana signaled a descent. She gently disengaged their hands.

"Slide down. Here. It is a gentle slope—have no fear. There are bushes below to catch us. Come, without thinking!"

With a swish, she was gone. Theora gulped and went after her, and Choria set herself into motion immediately after. She felt pebbles bruising her buttocks, switches of branches flicking against her face as she flew past them. Then she was stopping in a sneeze of dust and a tangle of shrubbery; others were sorting themselves out as she came to a halt.

"Crawl," muttered their guide. Choria dropped to hands and knees, then to her belly. Theora was beside her, and she checked her position by feel. The girl was learning, for there was little to correct in her attitude.

Amid a tickle of foliage, soft sounds of insects and

small creatures moving away from them, they crept forward after Petriana. Choria could hear water flowing, and not too distantly. A bird shrilled from overhead, an irritating sker-wee sker-weee! as it circled over the valley.

She set her hand on something that squirmed, serpentlike beneath it. Choria gasped and bit her lip. Snakes were not her favorite creatures—but this one had not bitten, being, most probably, as frightened as she.

She heard the twin of her gasp from Theora, just behind her. She tensed, ready to clap a hand over her mouth if she screamed, but there was no other sound. Choria felt a warm pride welling up in her. It had only been the possession of the power that had corrupted the Makra Theora. She was beginning to become an admirable person without it.

CHAPTER TWENTY-FOUR

They came out of dense brush into a cleared space. Petriana's warning hiss wasn't necessary, for both her companions knew that the clearing surrounded the sleeping spaces of the Searchers on duty here. Their eyes were used to the darkness, by now, and they picked their infinitely careful way around the dark bulks that were sleeping men, rolled into their blankets.

A voice sounded, off to their left. Another answered. Choria was sure that men had been set to watch the path leading to the road to the pass. No one had suspected any other way into the valley, just as Petriana had predicted.

They moved through the middle of the encampment. Except for snores and gruntings and curses muttered in sleep, there was no sound as they crept through. On the other side, where a pebbly surface patched with grass could be felt beneath her hands, Choria stopped again at Petriana's signal.

She could hear the woman rising, brushing away dust and twigs from her skirt. A firm hand came out of darkness and tugged her to her own feet. She pulled Theora up.

Fingers touched her face, turned it to her right. They stood beside a rough wall formed of logs and stone, just as Petriana had described it. Above, against the starred sky, loomed the crag from which the watchers must keep their vigil. There was the faintest of illumination touching the stones along the top of the wall.

"Watchers?" whispered Choria.

"Yes. There. Accessible from this direction." She led Choria along the wall to a stretch of scree that must have fallen from the height over long years. "You want to remove them?" It was the merest breath.

"Wait the count of five hundred, slowly. I will come then or not at all," the girl replied.

She moved up the loose rubble, taking care not to set any slipping behind her. Coming around an outcrop of stone, she heard voices and paused, listening to the sleepy murmur of talk. Two men. The words were unintelligible, but one set of footsteps came toward her. She slipped back around the stone and took her scarf into her hands.

There was a roomy shelf where she stood. As the man came around the narrow spot, she waited for his entire body to appear on her side against the warm light from the pen below. Then she whipped the versatile sash about his neck and pulled it taut, gave the extra tug and jerk that Bethor had taught her. The neck broke audibly.

She laid him silently onto the stony ledge and peered around the corner. The remaining watcher was huddled in a blanket, facing outward and slightly away from her position. His head nodded forward and was jerked upright twice as she watched. Good. He was sleepy. He glanced from time to time in the direction in which his companion had gone, as if expecting him to return. That was even better.

Choria went back as she had come, then walked forward, taking long strides, hearing the pebbles crunch beneath her boots. She walked around the rock as confidently as if she were returning to an assigned post—and then she rushed the remaining man, her blade in her hand. It stopped the warning cry in his throat with a gurgle. She wiped the metal on his blanket and returned to those waiting below.

They found the gate into the pen and she chopped it

loose with Theora's dagger. They slid through the narrow opening they had made and looked around. Three shapes were there, anonymous in their blankets.

"Bethor!" said Choria softly. "Bethor! We have come for you!"

Three sets of sleeping breaths stopped simultaneously. One of the figures rose, shedding its blanket onto the ground.

"It is...the Makra? Choria, it is really you?"

The familiar voice brought her to his side. "Be quiet. Yes. And Theora." She felt his start of astonishment. "And another whom you know. Come. The others can come, too, if they want."

He chuckled as they went to the gate. "Not they," he muttered. And even as he spoke the other two huddled into their blankets as if shunning the very sight of someone defying their captors.

They lost no time in leaving the valley along the track that was its only obvious entryway. Behind them, they left another pair of silent watchmen, though they merely stunned those and tied them with their own clothing, gagging them with their stockings, which Choria felt to be a very terrible, though deserved, punishment for their sins.

The track was little better than a game trail. It wound upward and downward, hugging the flank of the steep on the northwestern side of the valley. More than once they started a slide of rocks, which whispered and then thundered down, gaining noisiness with every yard of its progress.

Petriana was leading the procession, followed by Theora. Choria and Bethor came last, and he came slowly, haltingly, his breath whistling between his teeth. Choria knew him too well to believe his protestations that he was well and needed no help over the bad spots. She helped him anyway.

They had lagged well behind. Suddenly, in the blackness that was wheeling now toward dawn, they heard a choking cry, a struggle, the clang of metal on metal ahead of them. Forgetting weariness and injury, they rushed forward and then stopped.

There was the flare of torches beyond the roll of path before them. A voice was saying, "Well, My Lady Grandmother. How wonderful to find you safe after seeking for you so long. The Council will be most happy to learn of your continued well-being."

Choria looked up at Bethor. He was dimly illumined in the slight glow, and he nodded toward a tumble of rocks on the uphill side of the way. Together, they moved into hiding and listened to what was happening beyond their sight.

Petriana's voice was cool, amused, contemptuous. "Well, Grandson. How is it with the Heir of Algonath? Have you tricked the Council into thinking you a man of honor yet? Or are you still casting about frantically for some way of convincing them that you are what you are not?"

"You will convince them of that, Grandmother. Now I have you in my hands, and nothing will deter me. My uncle Kelldron, least of all."

"Kelldron! He employs idiots and trusts them. You need not worry your head about him. It is yourself who pose the problem, young Gerrold. You are a little man, unfit for rule. I will not help you. Let there be a Council of Rulership. That cannot help but choose a better man than you to rule here."

"You must speak for me. I am of the Blood. You are my kin. You cannot refuse. My grandfather would want you to."

"Your grandfather? He would spit upon me, if I did. He was all that you are not. Here! Where are you going with that young woman, scoundrel?"

There was the sound of a scuffle. "She drew steel upon

me! I have the right—"

"You have no right. She is my friend and my companion. Let her go. Come, child, to me. There. Now, Gerrold, tell me that you do not allow rapine among your men. I will not believe you, but tell me anyway."

There was the sound of movement, beyond the rise, going away from them, back toward the road.

But then, footsteps were also coming from behind! "Dongerre has followed us?" asked Choria in a whisper.

"Indeed. Come!" Bethor moved almost as lithely as he had before, and she supposed that he was forgetting his pain in the excitement of the moment. "Here, crouch down. When they pass, we must go through the entire mass of men. They will be so busy fighting and sorting things out that there will be confusion and to spare. You get Theora. I will attend to Petriana. We will run like the wind, whether it is possible or not."

She chuckled. How easily he had returned to the role of teacher and guide. How good it felt to have him there.

As they waited, hurrying steps crunched over the pebbles of the track. There was an exclamation of surprise. Then, "Attack!" someone shouted. In a moment, more men came running up the track and joined them.

The entire group charged over the hillock.

CHAPTER TWENTY-FIVE

Choria listened intently as yells erupted from the attackers, as well as those whom they surprised. There was the clang of steel on steel. The level of noise rose by the moment, and Bethor stood and moved forward, into the middle of the fray.

She had armed him with her own blade, retaining her short hunting knife and finding a stout stick. For close work, a good quarterstave was almost as good a weapon as any forged of metal. The two of them hit the rear of the struggling group without betraying any hint that they were not a part of the struggle.

Bethor was hewing his way toward Petriana, who was giving the two men set to guard her a considerable fight on her own. Choria found Theora tucked into a nook of rock, keeping out of the way but doing good work with a fist-sized stone she had found to substitute for her confiscated dagger.

She caught Choria's hand and was pulled from her hiding place like a cork from a bottle. Then they were moving through the grunting, bleeding press of men, leaving more cuts and lumps in their wake. They joined Bethor and Petriana on the downhill side of the melee, and the four of them kept low profiles as they scurried away in the tenuous light of dawn.

They reached the road to the pass in the misleading light that presages the coming of the sun. Bethor and

Petriana took the lead, though Bethor, the vigor of battle waning in him, was again moving painfully—more painfully than before.

The way upward was not a tempting one. Ragged clefts in the looming walls of stone showed where masses of soil and rock had come tumbling down into the narrow gully that was the road. This would be no simple matter of walking up a track and over a pass—it would require clambering up and down the least stable footing imaginable. Not once, but time after time. It would be slow and painful, especially for Bethor.

In addition, there would be pursuit, when those engaged in the fray on the path realized that their quarry was gone. The uncle and nephew might well join forces in pursuit of Petriana, intending to fight it out later for possession of her influential word.

Choria kept listening backward. The track was so narrow and so twisting that nobody could be seen, and she intended to hear any pursuer long before he might come into view. At last, she hurried ahead and tugged at Bethor's tunic.

"This will not do. They will be after us soon, and we cannot stay ahead of them, no matter what we do. I must lay a false trail—down and to the eastward. They probably expect Petriana will want to go back to Algon—why should she move into the land of her recent enemy? They have no idea who I might be, or Theora. You they know to be Sheratha, but they also know you to be friendly with Petriana.

"Hide yourselves in the first likely place you can find. I will brush away any trace of our passing as I go back. And then I will lay such a trail as a blind man might follow, misleading both those villains back into the valley."

Bethor grunted and lowered himself painfully onto a small stone. "It seems that I have taught you well, Makra Choria. If I were able, this would be the thing I would do.

Yet I mislike risking you...."

"And what am I? Of no value to anyone, Bethor. My father is gone; Garrier and your mother are gone. Except for you and Theora, I have no one left from the old life, and of the two of you, Theora can only think of me as the one who deprived her of the rule of Sherath. No, I am the one able to do this best, my old friend. And if I do not return, remember me kindly."

He reached to catch her hand. "More...than kindly," he said quietly. "Far more than kindly. Come back to us, Choria. I would give my right eye to be able to go with you."

She smiled, feeling a betraying warmth rise in her. But she turned away, after a last handclasp with Petriana and Theora. In ten heartbeats, she was out of their sight, watching the tumbled soil and rock carefully, removing any track that showed, any spot where a boot had scarred stone.

She paused a long while above the point at which the path led from the hidden valley into the road. She could see no movement, hear nothing but a confused commotion from beyond the first bend. At last, she hurried across and set about laying a trail not to be missed, even by villains who trusted fools.

She set her boots hard into any patch of dust she could find. She kicked at stones, scarring them with the metal-shod heels. Down she went, making all the disturbance she could manage, and going quickly, as well, for here the traveling was far easier than it was higher up. When the sun peered over the lower mountains to the east, she was down to the level of the better road, used in summer by herdsmen in taking their flocks and herds to the mountain pastures. She merged her track with that of a recently passed batch of goats, managing artistically to suggest that the goats had followed her along the way. Some yards along, she made a standing leap into the cropped grass edging the way, landing neatly and without marking the grass more than the goats had done before her.

She crept across the span of grass into the first of the long ranks of brushy growth. Sinking onto her stomach, she moved through that with little noise and less disturbance, until she was again near the point where the pass road converged with this lower way. There she waited, hidden so securely in the scrubby growth that even the birds soon went about their morning business again without noting her presence.

It was more than an hour before she heard the sound of her pursuers. She didn't risk moving enough to watch them go past, but she listened. Many feet. Curses and mutterings. Not disciplined troops, that was plain to her experienced ear. More of the scrapings, like the sons of Rentor, she felt certain.

The sun was overhead, now. The birds had settled into their midday quiet, and only the sounds of the moving men broke the silence. It took a long while for them to pass. She could only hope that they would find her traces on the main road and would follow them for a long time.

At last the noise died away. The untidy group was gone down the path, and she risked slipping along, still on her belly, to survey the way she must go. There was no sign of any watcher left on the track or of anyone bringing up the rear guard. She paralleled the path as long as it was possible, but when it narrowed to a cut between sheer stone walls she was forced down into it. Once more, she was infinitely careful, making sure not to overstep any tracks left by her pursuers. She kept to patches of rock or gravel. Where there were long spans of dust and soil, she walked backward, as lightly as possible.

By dark, she was level with that other path leading to the valley, but she kept going. Even in pitchy blackness, it was impossible to lose her way as long as the path was so well defined. Only when she came to the first of the rock slides did she stop. It was not sensible to keep on. A broken ankle would help no one, she knew, but she was anxious for those she had left behind.

Had they found a good place to conceal themselves? Had Gerrold's and Dongerre's men had the sense to send searchers both up and down the mountain? There were too many questions, none of which could have answers until morning.

She curled herself into a stony nook and let herself relax into sleep. Tomorrow would go as it would.

CHAPTER TWENTY-SIX

A clatter of stones woke Choria to the dimness of pre-dawn. Someone was coming down the perilous track, clambering over the tumbles of fallen stone. She stayed in her niche, waiting to see if this might be someone sent there by the enemy, though she felt in her bones that it must be one of her companions.

"Choria!" The name was breathed softly but with emphasis. "Are you here?" The words were followed by a troubled sigh, as the caller scrambled onto the path and moved down it. Theora!

"Here. Wait for me—there may be Searchers coming back this way soon. We'd best get up the mountain as quickly as we can." Her sister had whirled at the sound of her voice. Now she came forward and took Choria's shoulders into her hands.

"I...we were so worried! And Bethor was going mad. Hurry. He is itching to move from our camping place."

The two went up the rugged way with all possible speed, and by the time full light had come, they stood in a crevice where part of the sheer wall of stone had fallen long before. The pocket of soil revealed had nurtured a tiny grove of firs, and there they found Petriana sitting patiently and Bethor pacing the limited confines of the place like a caged bear.

He looked up as they came scrambling over the boulders. His smile warmed Choria all through. It seemed that

Bethor held her in esteem at least as great as that she felt for him. They said little, however. Choria picked up her own pack, left behind with her companions when she went on her mission, and they filed out of the grove onto the difficult trail.

Noon found them still struggling among slides of scree and tumbles of stones. Bethor was exhausted, Choria could tell, though he said nothing. His breath whistled between his teeth from time to time, and she ached to think of his battered body being put to such a test.

Petriana led still, being familiar with all the ways of her native mountains. Her memory seemed inexhaustible. She recalled the exact places where they might pull away debris to find a trickle of water. She was never deceived by branching ways that seemed to be trails at least as good as the one they followed. "That leads to a cul-de-sac," she would say. Or, "This is almost a way over the mountain's back, but it is blocked, some miles up, with a rock fall that cannot be passed."

They rested at last. Bethor was almost unable to move, and they massaged his battered limbs and fed him the best of the food they had scrounged in their flight from the rescue of Petriana.

While they sat in the shadow of an overhang, Choria asked the question she had been thinking over for a long while. "Petriana, are you going with us into Sherath? It is, after all, enemy country for now. Your home and family are here in Algonath. You are welcome, and more than welcome, to come, but I wanted to make certain that this is the thing you want for yourself."

The woman dusted grit from her clothing, then stretched her legs and sighed. "I have never been one to cling to matters that are lost. Algonath is a battleground between my grandson and his uncle. I refuse to be caught in the middle of that. I like you, Choria. I am beginning to see what Theora has it in her to become. I am fond of Bethor from old times. I will become a Sheratha, with your permission—and who has a better right to grant that? I will, if it suits her, attach my life to Theora's, as long as she needs someone to guide and advise her. It is my thought that you and Bethor may have plans of your own."

Their quick glances met in midair, then flicked apart. "There is no time to think of distant futures now," muttered Bethor. "Time for planning when we are safely out of these heights. Other dangers than your kinsmen's Searchers can be found here."

They groaned, rising to their feet, and started up again. It was only a short distance to the pass, and their track had been reduced to a narrow ledge with a sheer drop into impossible depths on the one hand and an overhanging cliff on the other.

Choria could see where great chunks of the way had fallen, leaving gaps in the perilous roadway that had to be jumped. She held her breath as Bethor cleared each one, and she noticed that Petriana always managed to be first over, having a ready hand to catch the injured man when he alighted. She set herself just behind him, hoping to catch him by some part of his clothing, if he should misjudge his launching.

Theora came behind her, uncomplaining. Choria felt that her sister understood what she was doing, and that feeling warmed her. In the years before, Theora had never looked outside herself to understand anything not directly connected to her own wants or needs.

They were over the pass by mid-afternoon, facing into the sun as they made their way down the mountain beyond the pass. Now their feet were on the soil of Sherath, for that pass marked the boundary between the two countries. There was, of course, no outpost set on such an inaccessible height, but Choria recalled that one was positioned at the joining of the main north-south road and the east-west one that came from the main pass. They would do well to avoid taking that road until they were well below the location of the guard post.

It took until nightfall to get down from that great height. Not only Bethor was suffering by the time they called a halt for the night; Choria felt as if her legs were dead weight, and her lungs burned from the altitude and exertion.

Nevertheless, she was the most fit of the four when they found a level spot in which to make a fire and to sleep without the danger of rolling down some decline. While the other three sank to the ground exhausted, she pulled herself up, in a short while, and set out for the tree line, which was in sight lower down. They needed wood for a fire and hot, cooked food. And not one of her companions was able to go that extra distance to reach the forest.

Luckily, the way was easier in the lower elevations. She made good time, going down, and within an hour she had a good load of wood slung across her back and tied with the invaluable sash. She could not spare her hands to carry an extra armful, for it would take the help of hands and arms to get up the steep trail again, burdened as she was. She had turned up the track, moved perhaps a dozen yards, when there came a sound behind her. She froze in her tracks, listening.

A low growl—off to her left and downhill. She turned slowly, carefully, drawing her blade at the same time.

The sun was almost down, sunk well behind the lesser mountains that straggled away to the west to meet the lower lands of her home. The forest was in deep shadow. But a deeper shadow stood in a clump of berry bushes, she thought. Something huge and dark. Something that growled.

She set her back against the first boulder of the trail. There was space to her left and right, between the last of the bushes edging the tree line and the beginning of the stony heights. She would see whatever charged from those bushes, if and when it decided that she might be possible prey.

It waited, as cautious, it seemed, as she. She settled herself against the rock and rested as well as she could while keeping a sharp watch. The last of the light left the sky, and stars sprang out brilliantly against the black depths. The pale stone would show that inky shape, she felt certain, for the starlight gave a certain dim definition to the area around her.

There was a call, far above; it echoed her name from the surrounding peaks. She didn't dare to reply—that might well trigger a charge in her unseen adversary. The growl was louder, now. The creature was approaching under cover of the brush. She would have—she mentally paced off the span of the pale stone—some twenty yards of time to respond to any attack from the last rank of bushes.

Adrenalin poured through her. She slipped the load of wood off her shoulder and went into a crouch, her blade ready.

The thing had to be a Great Bear of the Mountains. She had seen one, once, dead. The forester who had killed it had not lived to brag of it, but his fellows had brought the huge body into the city to show to their Makralo. She knew that her light blade would be as deadly as a needle to that mass of flesh and muscle, but it was all she had.

She felt almost disembodied. Death was coming uphill toward her, and she found herself strangely ready to meet it. There in the starlight, in the clean chill of the high lands, fined to the bone with her efforts of the past years, she realized that she had nothing to regret. Relinquishing her powers had been a healthful thing, leaving her spirit cleansed.

Bethor—her eyes filmed for a moment with unshed tears. Yet that had only been a possibility, unrealized and unspoken. She could not regret what she had never possessed. She blinked hard, and in the dimness she could see the bushes quiver as something huge moved through them. She braced herself, drew a deep breath.

To the remote gods of her people, she breathed, "Care for those I have loved. Protect them. Keep Theora true to what she can become!"

And then the growl became a roar, and the bear charged from the bushes across the pale stone.

Choria shrieked back. *"Choria!"* she cried. It had been her war cry, and that of her adherents.

Then the beast was upon her.

CHAPTER TWENTY-SEVEN

"Choria!"
"Choria!"
"Choria!"

Three voices were shouting out the cry. Choria was too busy thrusting at the swiping paws, avoiding the reaching head and the teeth that shone even in the darkness, to find time to wonder at such a variety of echoes.

There was a glimmer of light from the path to the pass, and she could see something moving behind the beast's side.

"Whuff!" said the creature in a surprised tone. It half - turned to see what had attacked its flank, and Choria took the opportunity to thrust beneath the suddenly vulnerable jaw, upward through the head—into the brain.

The entire tremendous body leaned backward against her, then collapsed on top of her. With a sigh of relief at having the thing done and over with, Choria fainted for the first time in her life.

She woke to find her head in Petriana's lap. There was a fire crackling at her side, and she looked about to find herself in the forest. Firs, their trunks warmed with the firelight, loomed above the spot where the camp was set. Bethor and Theora sat beyond the fire, watching her intently.

She moved an arm, experimentally. Pain shot through her from bruised muscles, but the limb moved to her command. Smiling up at Petriana, she accepted the woman's help in sitting upright. "My ribs!" she gasped.

"Nine hundredweight of bear fell upon them," Bethor said, his tone dry. "You cannot expect to feel as if you'd sustained the fall of a feather. Is there any sharp pain when you breathe?"

She knew that he was thinking of broken ribs that might do internal damage. She inhaled cautiously. The ribs hurt infernally, but there was no sharp, piercing pain. She shook her head. Legs obeyed her commands with only minor protests. Both arms felt as if lined with fire, but they worked. She looked about at her companions.

"I think I have been extremely lucky," she said. "But it is going to be hard to go all the miles we still have to cover to get to Sherath. If, that is, we are going there?"

Before anyone could reply, she realized how strangely her rescue had come. "How did you make it down the mountain?" she asked. "You were all too tired to move. And how did you contrive a torch? There was nothing up there to make one out of."

Bethor laughed. "I recall a day when you were wounded and carried back behind the lines. The first time I looked up, there you were, plying your blade left-handed. You are not the only one able to rise to an emergency. And as for the torch—why Petriana sacrificed a petticoat. No great mystery there." Then he sobered. "But we do need to determine our destination. Being who and what you are, you and Theora cannot go wandering about without the danger of being recognized."

Theora lifted her head, her eyes wide and suddenly frightened. "I have much to answer for," she whispered. "Do you think—do you think that the people will want to put me to death?"

Choria sat even straighter. "I know our people. They may become angry. They can do petty things, commit small crimes, but their hearts are sound. And they admire courage beyond anything else. I believe that I know how to make our country safe for you, Theora. Yet there is a risk—a tremendous one. It will be your decision...."—and she outlined, there in the flickering light amid the fir trees, the plan that had come to her in a flash of inspiration.

When she was through, Bethor was looking at her with approval. Petriana was regarding Theora speculatively. Theora was staring into the fire, her face terribly pale. She said nothing for a long time. Then she looked up at her sister and gazed into her eyes for another lengthy while. Her expression was unreadable, and Choria waited for her answer without any clue as to what it might be.

"I will do it," she said in a quiet voice that held traces of great strain. "If I live, or if I die, I will do it. It is only...just...." Her last word was almost inaudible.

"Then we will go toward Sherath," Choria said, looking about the group, "if that is agreeable to all here."

Bethor rose painfully and came to sit beside her. He took her bruised hand into his no-less-bruised one. "We will follow the Makra Choria gladly," he said.

There was no dissent.

CHAPTER TWENTY-EIGHT

They rested in the high forest for three days. That time gave both Bethor and Choria an opportunity to work the worst of the pain from their bruised bodies, as well as to heal various cuts and abrasions. Theora and Petriana hunted for small game, and their luck was good, or their skill was greater than anyone had suspected, for they came in each night with conies or ground squirrels or fat burrowers to roast over the fire.

With fresh meat to go with the remnants of their dried stuff, all three regained their energies quickly. On the fourth day they were ready to go down again into the land of the Sheratha and to find what might await them there.

The path through the forest was steep, but the homed beasts used it regularly. The footing was good, and there were bushes to steady the worst of the descents, where snowmelt had eroded the very rock into tiny cliffs.

They were down that height fairly soon. And from there they could follow the meandering streams that worked their way down to the lower country, cutting their courses in the easiest ways around the toes of the intervening mountains.

In three more days, they stood on the great plain of Sherath, looking away westward toward the river and the still-invisible city. They could see the road, with the guard post.

"We will not go there. I have no idea who mans it

now, and I would like to find friends who will stand with us, before making ourselves known in the city. To be brought there as captives would not be a positive thing," Choria said, as they debated their next course.

Bethor agreed, much to Theora's relief, and Petriana nodded. So they went out into the grasslands and across the plowed and sprouting fields only after darkness had fallen. They crossed the road in blackness, and nobody was there to hear them go.

Then it was a clear run toward the farms along the river. They camped for the rest of the night in a clump of trees. In the morning, they could see the normal flow of incomers to the city moving up the southward road.

Theora accepted Bethor's battered hat as a disguise and pulled it well down over her forehead. With her boy's clothing, she looked more like a stripling than ever. Choria could do little—but she was not abhorred in Sherath.

The four joined a group that had gone aside to rest in a field. There was little talk, for the farmer folk were a bit shy about approaching this city that had loomed so near to their lives, yet had been so remote from their experience.

They moved in silence along the dusty road, sometimes passing other groups, sometimes giving way to them. From time to time, horsemen came pounding down the way, and most of these were in the colors of the Guard. Choria avoided looking directly at them as they passed, for fear some one of them would recognize her before she was ready.

"We cannot go to the House," she said to Bethor, as they drew near the gates. "It is tumbled into ruin, and I am certain that no one has wanted to rebuild it. Where might we go until we are ready to reveal ourselves?"

"My father's house will be standing. My cousin Raynolt survived our ill-fated campaign, though he was crippled. For that reason he...was not sent to war with the rest of us. He lives there, I am sure, with his wife Orsala and their children. We can find shelter there."

They moved through the streets amid the modest scatter of people. Some of the houses had been damaged and were under repair. There were fewer goods shops, and those goods were less fine than they had been before. But Sherath was surviving and prospering as well as might be. Choria felt proud of her people. They had not given up, no matter what occurred in their city and country.

Garrier's house was marked with a falcon in flight, a well-forged metal sculpture that hung from thin chains, moving gently above the doorway in the breeze funneled down the street. Choria looked up at it with affection.

Bethor opened the garden gate, and the party filed through and heard it close behind them with a certain relief. Here they were not open to public scrutiny, as they touched the brazen bell hanging beside the door.

There was the sound of uneven footsteps inside. The door opened a crack, and a gray eye peered through it. "What do you want here?" asked a gruff voice. "We've little enough, and none for those who'll not work for their own."

"Raynolt! What a welcome to your kin!" Bethor laughed. "Not to mention the Makra and our guest!"

The door swung open in a swish of wood against stone flagging. A big fellow beyond it dropped his crutch and caught his cousin about the shoulders. "We were sure that you were dead in some distant Algonath field, unknown and unmourned," he said. "But young Eldon maintained stoutly that his uncle Bethor could not be killed by any number of soldiers, in Algonath or any place else. It appears he was right. He usually is, come to think of it. Shows some traces of the power." Raynolt looked shyly at Choria. "There was a kinship, long ago."

"Make certain that he learns to control it and to know that it does not make him any more important than his fellows," the girl said, her tone solemn. "It can be...dangerous."

Now came Orsala, asking who was come, and then the children descended upon the new arrivals with questions and exclamations.

The odd glances cast at Theora changed a bit as their tale unfolded, but there was still a wariness among those in the house. They recalled all too well the disastrous time of her reign. Thinking it a good time to introduce the subject, she outlined her plan. Raynolt and his wife listened intently, nodding from time to time, as she talked.

"That will expiate the guilt as nothing else could possibly do," said Orsala, when she was done. "But it will be dangerous. There are many who have lost much. There are bitter folk here, where before there were none. Is she willing to risk it?'

Theora looked straight into her eyes. "I am," she said.

CHAPTER TWENTY-NINE

The former Makrala of Sherath stood upon the ancient platform, a half step above the level of the cobbled street. The street was full of people, and no guard stood near.

In a borrowed window above, Choria watched her sister, who stood straight, chin up, waiting for the first of those who would come to the judging. Only her impassioned plea had saved Theora from instant death, once it was known who she was. And only Choria's own status as one beloved of the people had allowed her the chance to speak.

Indeed, it had been Bethor, one of their own, highly respected, who had gained his Makra the right to speak at all. Since that day, the tongues of the Sheratha had never stilled. The judging of the former Makrala was in the forefront of every mind above the age of ten.

Raynolt had been correct—there was more bitterness in the city than had ever existed before. Greed and vanity had been common enough, but no citizen had had cause to complain of injustice from those who ruled him.

Choria's heart was thumping with suspense. It was a chancy thing, she knew. The people were not quite those she had known and understood for all her life. That change might well mean that she had condemned her sister to death.

There had been times when that would have been a very good thing, but Theora was as different from her old

166

self as her people were different from themselves. Now there was hope for her.

A short, stout man stepped forth from the crowd and looked up at her window. He touched his cap politely but without undue reverence. "If the Makra will allow?" he asked.

Choria could not imagine what he wanted to say. Such a thing had never happened at a judging. But she nodded her consent, then said, "I have no right to stop you, Anzil. I am only a citizen here now, even as you."

He stood, sturdy legs well apart, his stocky shape reared back so that he could look at her. Though he was red with shyness, he spoke at last.

"Makra Choria, we have known that you had no thought of ruling here in our dear city. We know that you and your betrothed have said that you would live apart, in the forest to the west. Yet that is a thing that we cannot imagine allowing you to do. We need you. Your family has, with few exceptions, kept Sherath safe and prosperous." He paused to wipe his steamy brow with a pink kerchief.

"Those of us whom your father chose to help him administer the city have talked together, since your request on your return. It has not been easy to reach a consensus. But we have a proposal for you, the justice of which we feel you cannot deny."

She looked down into his earnest eyes, feeling in her bones the terrible sacrifice that she was about to be asked.

"If you and Bethor will consent to rule here, as did your father and all the Makraitis for many generations, we will allow your sister her judgment. We will think of the change that can be seen in her behavior and her attitude. This may seem a harsh request, tainted with blackmail, but we are a desperate people. We have proven to ourselves that we lack the balanced knowledge and judgment to plunge into self-rule."

He wiped his brow again. "In time, given training in all the things that you know better than we, it is possible that we may become wise enough for that. For now, we need a leader. We need you. Will you consent?"

Choria reached for Bethor's hand, grateful for his warm presence beside her. They had so longed for a life in the forest, without the complication of human needs compelling them. She looked up into his eyes.

"Of course, we must," he murmured, moving his lips without using his voice.

She looked down into the street again. "Anzil, we will do as you ask. Deal...gently...with my sister."

He touched his cap again. "For myself, I will. I cannot speak for all. Yet I feel that justice, whatever it may be, will come of this judging. Thank you, Makrala Choria."

Simply as that, Choria became Makrala, without any ceremony or ritual, and by the will of her people. Her eyes filled with tears as she watched the first-comer lift the spear from its socket and touch it to her sister's throat.

One by one, the people passed. Three hundred times the spear was lifted, touched, set again into its place. As the crowd thinned, Theora seemed to tire. Choria could see her shoulders drooping, yet she made no complaint. As confidently as their father had ever done, she endured the judgment, which she had sworn to eliminate.

When it was done, Choria went down to help her from the platform with her own hands.

Those who had taken part had not gone away, remaining at some distance until the ceremony was completed. Now they came again into the space before the ruined House of Makraitis. As Theora stepped firmly from the platform, a timid cheer arose. Choria had been correct. The Sheratha admired courage, in whomever it might occur.

Choria took Theora's hand in her left and Bethor's in her right. She turned to face the largest group, and the crowd surged about her. "Has she paid her debt to you?"

she asked.

Anzil stepped forward again. "If she continues as she has begun, she will have paid her debt," he said.

"Then we shall serve you as well as we can for as long as we are needed. Yet be informed—never again will the power of the Makraitis be allowed to grow unchecked. It is a thing that can corrupt those who possess it. Without it, Theora would, I devoutly believe, never have become a peril to her people. That power has been laid aside.

"If it shows itself in our children, we shall control and train it—or we will eliminate it." She looked about at her people.

"Never again will a Makraitis be tortured by something inside herself or himself. Never again will one, like our uncle, be forced into death in trying to cope with the terrible thing he inherited from his forefathers. It is not power that is needed in a ruler. It is wisdom." She smiled up at her betrothed. "And love.

"May the gods permit us to have both."

They turned, as Petriana took Theora's hand to follow them. The Sheratha cheered them all the way to Garrier's house, and when the door closed behind the last of them, they went away smiling. Sherath was once more in the hands of those who used her well.

CHAPTER THIRTY

Choria, even amid the bustle of her marriage to Bethor and the myriad duties of being Makrala, found time to keep a close watch upon her sister. She had found a house for Theora and Petriana, and the two had settled in together far more amicably than anyone would have expected. Petriana, being the wife and mother of rulers, had the assurance necessary for dealing with Theora on a daily basis.

Theora herself, to Choria's surprise, grew almost timid. It was as if, without her power, knowing herself to be physically weak and morally guilty, she had become afraid to face even the limited world of Sherath.

When a delegation came from the Heir of Algonath, asking for the return of his grandmother, Choria had called upon Petriana. "Do you want to go?" she asked the older woman.

Petriana smiled. "I will not be a pawn in anyone's game. I much prefer my present occupation. When our pretty lady tires of being a reclusive penitent, she will find something more amusing to do. One day, she will learn what effect her beauty has upon young men. Then, I believe that you will need me badly. That is a power even more intoxicating than that of the Makraitis."

Choria laughed. "I had not thought of that. You are more than welcome to remain. I will make use of your years and experience, from time to time, if you have no objection. You have seen much and learned more. But I would take it kindly if you told the delegation, yourself, of your decision. Relations between our countries are still sensitive, and I wouldn't have them think that I am detaining you against your will."

Petriana had no difficulty persuading the delegation that she had no intention of returning to her grandson's tender attentions. They left with rather more speed than they had come to Sherath, leaving that lady relieved of some harsh words she would have preferred to say directly to her grandson.

Theora did, indeed, learn, in time, that beauty is almost as potent as power. And, young men being famous for recklessness, she did not lack for suitors, though she never chose to marry one of them.

Instead, she became an indulgent aunt to Choria and Bethor's children. She even, to her sister's private amusement, took up the care of the poor, and before her life ended was blessed among them as a very angel of tenderness and concern.

So Sherath prospered again, and if the Makraitis Gift was lost to the Sheratha, they never missed it. The bitterness dwindled away to nothing, and once more the city was a place of smug contentment.